CORPUS

C.L. Kelley

Crystal Lake Entertainment
www.CrystalLakePub.com

"C.L. Kelley is an exciting new voice in horror. *Corpus* is an epic tale of the paranormal, building lore I hope to see expanded on. Dark, gritty and compelling, with stellar pacing and a new and intriguing take on the sub-genre. Highly enjoyable."

— Laurel Hightower, author of *The Day of the Door*

Torrid Waters is the pulp and extreme horror imprint of Crystal Lake Entertainment. For this book, the author has supplied these trigger warnings: animal death, graphic violence, body horror, misogyny, religious mania, domestic violence, suicide, being unhoused, and cannibalism.

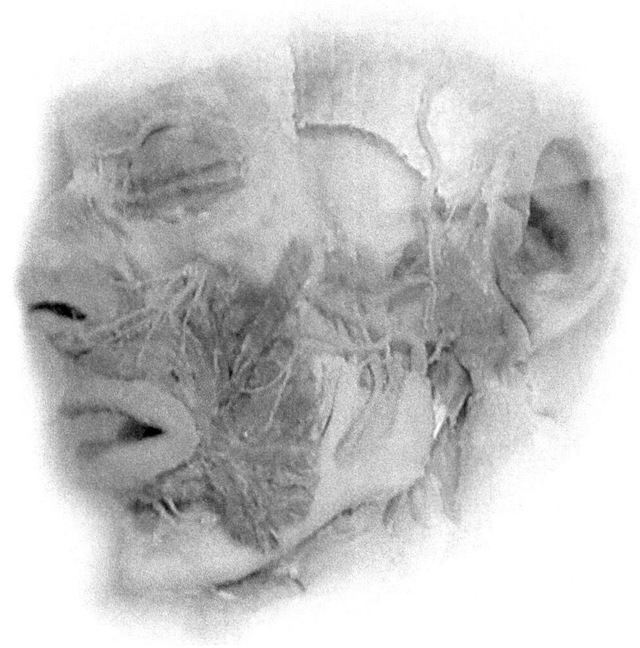

ONE

The house had been decaying for more than thirty years now. Its royal blue paint first faded, then peeled away entirely, like desiccated skin. The exposed woodwork grayed and warped under the beating of weather and negligence.

Many of the windows were shattered, though only a few by vandals. The last boy who approached the house, emboldened by his friends and rock in fist, got no closer than twenty yards before he found himself inexplicably weeping, weeping so hard that he was on the verge of retching. He retreated, unable to articulate to his baffled and shaken peers what had evoked such dread and sadness in him.

Now only the occasional storm-blown branch braved the ruined façade, though sometimes it seemed that even nature itself was loath to violate the house's territory.

Animals avoided the place. But every once and a while a nearby bird or rat or stray dog would stiffen, come to attention as if hearing a silent call. Ignoring the mad, shrill warnings of its pack, the animal would wander toward the house as if in a trance, disappear through a ragged crack, and never reemerge. At first, only small things answered the call: flies, spiders, lizards, birds. Then rats, buzzards, cats. Eventually, sickly dogs or mangy raccoons came, their resolve weakened by injury or illness. The voice grew stronger, increased its radius, falling over the woods in a subliminal shroud.

The house stood in mostly country, separated from neighbors by several acres of overgrown trees, hidden crab-like in its shell of vegetation. No one had attempted to approach it for sale, quantify it with campfire stories of chain-clanking ghosts, or spread rumors of brutal hatchet murders. It was as if there were a house-shaped black hole in the minds of anyone who came too near it. And that was just as things had been planned, because there was still time needed. But not much more. So the veil of secrecy was slowly dropped, enough that some, but not all, would start to notice it again. And maybe the next young boy who came with a rock in his fist, or a wanderer with a need for shelter from a rainstorm, wouldn't be wise enough to run. Then the house would be ready.

So the year slid into autumn, birds flew to their deaths on the panes of jagged glass, and if anyone passed too close to the house, they might feel a light touch on their backs, and a whisper of invitation in their ears.

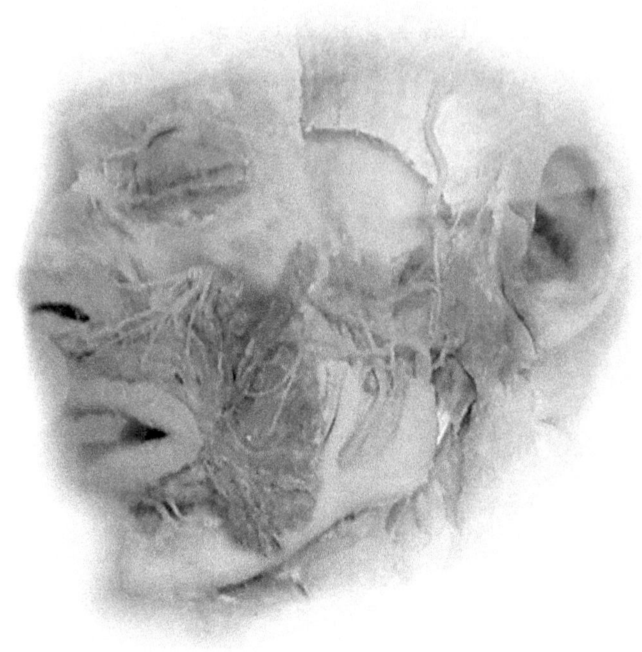

TWO

The girl sitting across the bus aisle from Orin had been coughing since Market Street. Not discreet coughs into a tissue, either, but body-wracking hacks, the kind people get when they have a case of untreated pneumonia. And Orin thought she *looked* sick, with her pinched, chalky face and sunken eyes. She wore a striped polo shirt, the collar dark and stiff with grime, along with frayed denims and bargain-bin sneakers held together with silver duct tape. Around her emaciated frame she had wrapped a brown leather car coat, a size too big and cracked with age. Though her obvious illness made it hard to judge her age, Orin thought she was probably in her early twenties. Riding the bus at night was always the best way to see people like her, the dregs of existence. If you made a couple of loops around town, you would see dozens of them, scrambling into their pockets for enough to afford the ride, settling their pathetic bones into the cracked leather seats.

She might truly be sick, but Orin thought it more than likely that she was a drug addict, collapsing into the final stages of meth or crack abuse or whatever other filth she put into her body. She had to be, to look that bad that young. She probably put a lot of other disgusting things into her body, too—disgusting things she did for money.

Orin's skin crawled as he thought of all the diseases she had by now, either by drugs or sex. Just like all the others he'd found, the six whose filth he'd taken from the world forever. Orin caressed the freshly oiled and sharpened bayonet in its special sheath under his coat and took a long, ragged breath. Soon it would be seven.

Only six? Orin felt like he'd been killing them forever, a man squishing an infinite tide of cockroaches under his heel. Had it only been nine months since he'd first shoved Grandfather's old Army bayonet into that screaming mouth, the one with the missing tooth that stank of cheap gas station wine? Sure, the garbage Orin eliminated might have been hiding in plain sight, might have just looked to other people like transients or homeless people down on their luck, but Orin knew what they really were. They were whores that did stuff for money, whores that wanted to take the pureness out of him, take the Jesus out of him and make him forever filthy like them. He wouldn't let them put that sin in him anymore. And he would keep going until the Lord God Almighty's one and only precious Son came to him and said that he was all healed, that he was saved and pure and sanctified again.

As if magically acknowledging Orin's will, the girl stood up to get off at the next stop. She hobbled down the aisle before stepping out into the night. He followed, but at a safe distance. Not that the girl would notice; she seemed so lost in her own sickness that she probably wouldn't have given him a second glance if he had been kicking at her heels. She shuffled along, huddled in her raggedy coat, stopping only when her body convulsed with coughing. She walked past neon doorways booming with music and violent voices, past sidewalk people smoking and screeching into cell phones, until she wandered into the quieter streets of the city that always seemed steeped in darkness, where in the distance a siren always wailed and a chorus of mongrel dogs howled in counterpoint.

Maybe she was looking for a place to sleep, since this part of the city wasn't a stranger to derelict buildings. *A squatter,* Orin thought, but that word and the image it conjured up made Orin want to gag, and he hurried his step, eager to close in and use the knife. Probably, she was looking for an empty room in one of those abandoned buildings so she could turn her tricks, so she could let dirty homeless men grunt on top of her for a sip of rotgut wine or a crumpled dollar bill. She would probably even let them put it in her rectum, and Orin knew only whores and sodomites let that happen, just as surely as he knew that one day Jesus would laugh while watching all of them burn in Hell.

She turned off the main street into an alley, and he closed the distance between them, walking on the balls of his feet so the quickening tap wouldn't give him away. He rounded the lip of the alley mere seconds after she had, and his hand was already gripping the hard, smooth wooden hilt of the bayonet.

Orin searched for her in the gloom among the bags of trash and hulking dumpsters, but he couldn't find her. Had she really moved that fast? Was she already curled behind one of the dumpsters? Slightly confused, Orin drew the bayonet and stepped further into the alley, trying to listen for the girl's giveaway cough, and letting his eyes adjust to the deeper darkness. Pushing down his bewilderment, he knew the cough would soon give her away, and then he would be ready. His breath quickened into a pant. Soon, soon the whore would—

A tremendous force shoved Orin from behind, sprawling him onto the wet pavement of the alley and knocking his breath from him in a cold snap of shock.

Though startled, Orin somehow managed to retain his hold on the blade. He scrambled on the wet pavement of the alley and felt a pain in his knee when he tried to find his balance. What was happening? He thought she must have gotten behind him somehow and shoved him, but he'd seen her go into the alley, and there was no place she could have hidden to slip past him. Besides, no way could a sickly girl knock Orin off his feet like that. He had a foot of height on the girl and was easily twice her size.

Orin whirled around, the bayonet held in front of him as he tried to search out his attacker. He couldn't see anything, but then he squeezed his eyes to clear the ringing in his head, and he saw her. Somehow, despite all logic, the girl had maneuvered behind him.

Fine, she'd gotten in a lucky shove, but now he was going to make her regret it. Wordlessly, he took a step forward, but almost immediately, he came to an abrupt halt. The ringing in his head had stopped long enough for him to take in what was different about the girl now. She no longer hunched over like a withering grandmother, but instead stood straight with shoulders back, her statue-still body no longer wracked with coughs. Her hands were in the pockets of her coat, and though her eyes were still lost in the shadows of sunken pallor, they caught the light and glittered like shards of broken wine bottles.

"Now," she said in a sandpaper voice, "just what did you have in mind to do with that?"

Before he could respond, an invisible force seized Orin, slamming him against the wall hard enough to make black flowers bloom in his vision. Though the physical source of this power remained obscured, he could feel it on him, wet and slimy and strong like great tentacles, and being touched by it made him sick and ashamed. The invisible tentacles dragged him up along the wall until Orin found himself suspended six feet from the alley pavement. He tried to scream, but something cold and invisible shoved itself into his mouth, making him gag.

He heard the slap of the girl's dilapidated shoes as she strolled toward him. She stopped at his feet and looked up, saying, "This just won't do. Why don't we get a little closer?"

There was a meaty pop like breaking bone, and suddenly the girl wasn't there. Orin's eyes went wide in disbelief, his grasp on reality as he understood it slipping away. A rush of hot, foul air hit his face, and the girl was inches from him, floating and grinning with a mouth of yellow teeth so numerous they threatened to split her cheeks open.

Orin realized he could no longer feel the cold and slimy pressure on his mouth, and that he could talk and draw breath again. He stammered, "Wh-what are you?"

The knife was wrenched from his hand and hovered in front of him, a black steel wasp seeking a target. Instead of answering him, the girl said, "You're such a scared little man. Exactly what I was looking for..."

The bayonet moved toward his eye with cruel, teasing slowness. He tried desperately to move his head, but the invisible hands held him still. Though his head was immoveable, he could still scream. The tip of cold steel that he himself had so lovingly sharpened pierced his eye, and Orin bellowed in pain and fear. Through the vision of the eye that was left, he saw the girl grin, a grin that grew wider and wider, a grin that held sharp, innumerable teeth. And then she moved toward him, as slow and cruel as the blade, but the blackness beyond those yellow teeth, the blackness that would soon swallow him, was much worse.

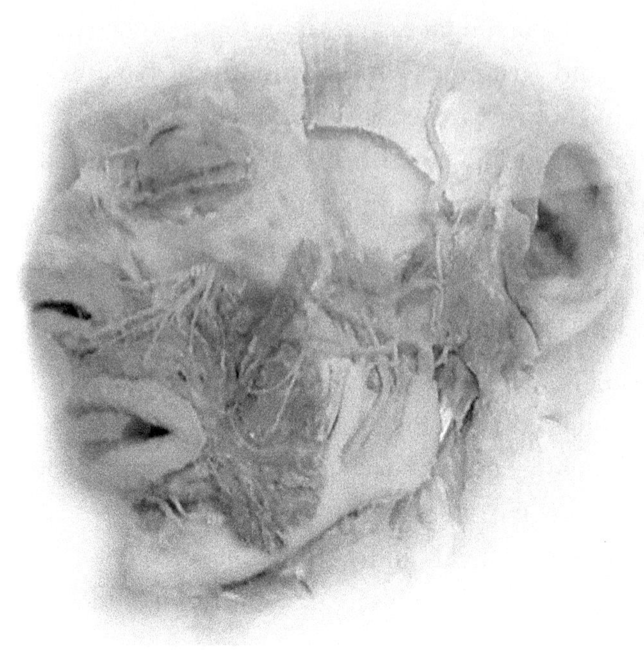

THREE

The man who lived at 17 Hibbing Street was luckier than most of the others. He could pass for human, even upon second glance. For all appearances he was a normal, stoop-shouldered man in his early fifties with thinning hair. His skin had a gray pallor, and his eyes were very dark, but most people weren't around him long enough to notice the wrong things. That he cast no shadow, and that his reflection in mirrors appeared as distorted as that viewed in carnival glass, and that it sometimes seemed to move on its own. Even if someone had been observant enough to notice, the man would have only to speak a few words with the would-be sleuth, reach into his pulpy little brain and give it a tweak. It was no effort for him. He could make someone kill their own family and then eat a handful of broken glass if he wanted to. Adjusting memory was nothing—just another advantage he had over others. Not that he'd ever known many like him.

It wasn't from lack of trying. He kept his ear to the ground—or, rather, his informants kept *their* ears to the ground—for anything that might alert him to any…*potential competition.* He'd lived in many different cities throughout the years, and he occasionally caught wind of someone like him, but they were merely passing through, gone as soon as they had come. The few who had tried to burrow down and set up a more permanent dwelling, who had tried to encroach on his territory, he'd killed. It helped immensely to have agents who could go out in the daylight.

Through the patter of the rain outside, the man was roused by a knock on his door. Luckily, it was someone he'd been expecting, or his caller would never have gotten this close. He opened the door to the soft spray of rain, his porch light illuminating a burly figure in a slicker.

"Good evening, Detective Simmons," the man said in a voice as sonorous as church bells.

The detective stepped through reluctantly, his eyes drifting to the cluttered living room and the man's eyes followed, taking in his lair again with a pride that never seemed to fade. An overstuffed green armchair was nestled among a mountain of trinkets, mementos, and *bric-a-brac.* Gold figurines gleamed dully next to framed family photos and children's toys. Sagging shelves behind him were crammed with fine, leather-bound first editions, sentimentally thumbed paperbacks, and yearbooks stretching back to the 1940s. Lining the mantle of his cold fireplace were numerous urns.

The man settled back into his armchair like a dragon resting on top of his mountain of plunder. "What do you have for me tonight?" he asked.

The man had touched the detective's mind enough times now their exchange required little effort. Simmons rattled off a debriefing of the city's hidden news, the things that didn't make it into the papers. But when he spoke about a murder that had already featured in the morning edition, the man reached into the detective and seized his vocal cords.

"Is there a reason you're telling me this?" he asked. When Simmons didn't answer, he remembered to return the detective's ability to speak.

Simmons continued in a measured tone. "There were certain aspects of the case that were not reported in the newspapers. Things you told me to pay attention to."

"Such as?" The man flexed his long fingers with a dry crack.

"The victim, Orin Winslow, was murdered in an alley downtown. The papers reported that he had been stabbed to death, which is mostly true. But we found him pinned to the wall, impaled by lead pipes and pieces of scrap metal, even an old Army bayonet—all of it driven right through the brick. We did tests on the bayonet and found it consistent with the murder weapon used in the recent killings of a few female derelicts. We thought perhaps Orin was the latest victim and that the killer had changed their pattern, but when we investigated his apartment, we found…*souvenirs* of the other victims."

The man's long fingers drummed the mahogany arm of his heavy chair. "That's intriguing, but I'm still waiting for why it's a special kind of interesting."

"Mr. Winslow was impaled twenty feet off the ground."

The tension passed from the man like a summer storm. He smiled. "You've done very well, Detective Simmons," he said, his voice on the verge of bubbling with laughter. The man stood up and walked toward the detective. Even with his stooped shoulders, he towered over Simmons by half of a foot. "I'm pleased by your news. But I still require a tribute."

The detective dug into his overcoat pocket and produced an intricately banded diamond ring. It wasn't gaudy, but it was still a clearly expensive piece of jewelry. When the man went to take it from the detective's fingers, he encountered a slight resistance, but then he reached into Simmons's mind and found the right thing to squeeze to make him release his grip.

"Your wife's ring?" he asked.

The detective nodded, adding, "It's a family heirloom. It belonged to her grandmother."

"Perfect," the man purred, slipping the ring onto his right pinky finger. "And what are you going to tell her when she tells you she lost it?"

The detective began with a hitch in his voice, "I'm going to tell her I'm glad she lost it, that I've been thinking I don't want to be married to her anymore." Simmons breathed heavily after finishing the sentence, as if he'd just run a mile, and his eyes were moist.

The man smiled in satisfaction, but he wasn't done. "And the next time you get into an argument with your son Andrew, your so-very-willful son, what are you going to do?"

Tears spilled down the Detective Simmons's face, but he still spoke in a monotone. "I'm going to hit him."

"And?" the man insisted.

"And I'm going to tell him that I'm ashamed to be his father."

"Very good, Detective Simmons," the man said, holding out the hand that now gleamed with the diamond ring. The detective fell painfully to his knees and kissed the ring with the reverence of a man meeting a pontiff, and his hot, tear-dampened face wet the cold hand.

Simmons left without another word, and the man followed him onto the porch. As the police officer's Crown Victoria pulled away into the night, a large crow alit onto the railing, letting out a throaty caw. The man held out his forearm for the crow, who dutifully hopped on, digging its black talons into the sleeve of his wool cardigan.

"And what news do you have for me, little one?" he asked, staring into the bird's obsidian eyes.

With people he could push ideas and demand information, but not truly retrieve thoughts telepathically. With the simple minds of animals, however, it took so little effort that he might as well call it mind-reading. They thought not in words, but in images, sensations, and sounds, and the man usually had no trouble interpreting them. He was not only a good talker but a good listener as well.

From the mind of the bird, he saw a house in the woods, a

dark place as hungry and indiscriminate as the man himself. So, there were two forces to contend with tonight. Two forces he must dissect, understand, and rein in, if necessary.

"Now that's *very* interesting," he said, and stroked the black bird's glossy head.

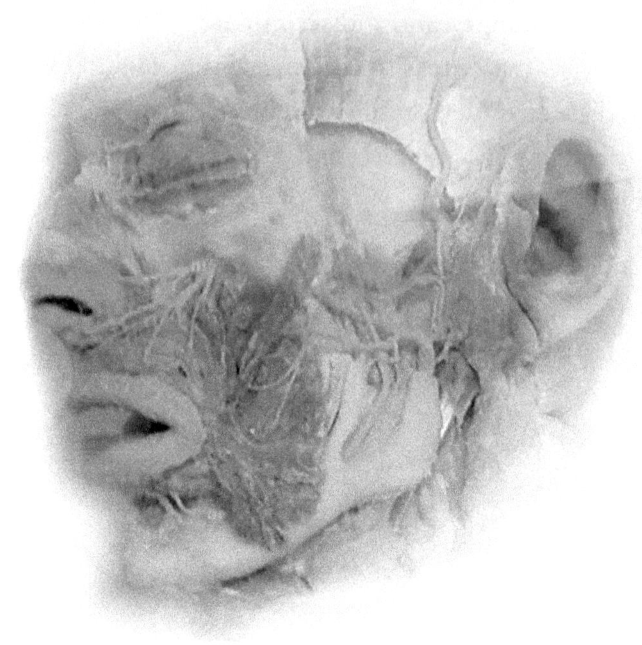

FOUR

Change. Flux. Transformation.

These were words the drifter in the battered denim jacket knew well—words imprinted on every mote of his being. He was acutely aware of his body: every bone, muscle, and sinew. Of how it was supposed to be when he was shaped like a man, and how it could change. He could run as swiftly as a hound when he went onto four legs, could take to the sky on vast and leathery wings, or even scatter the atoms of his body into a fine mist.

He knew when transformation came. And so tonight he knew exactly when his body responded to the scent, when it signaled to him that things were about to change.

The man in denim never stayed in one place for too long. And fortunately, safety for him was easily obtained. A hole in the ground, a cave, the crawlspace in an abandoned building: all sufficed to meet his needs for rest. But unlike some of the others, he was not one for subtlety, and if he stayed in one area for too long, people would inevitably come hunting for him. Maybe not him specifically—he knew enough now to know that people these days didn't readily grasp what he was—but they would want some answers for their mutilated livestock and eviscerated citizens. So he moved like a shark, never daring to stop, and when he passed time resting, with a brain no longer capable of dreams, he was always poised for the run.

When he came to this current town, though, he immediately sensed that things were different here. Perhaps, he thought, he had been headed here all along, drawn to this source by a weak but inexorable pull. He made his way by cover of night among the ramshackle houses and rickety country store, the sad excuse for a town square, passed it all by until he made it to the all-too-eagerly encroaching forest. There he took a form more suited to fast travel, a grotesque and hairless shape that had four legs and could almost be called a wolf.

In this less-than-human form, the signal called out to him even more strongly, and he could sense just how pervasive it was, like a psychic net cast over the whole area, dragging in different lifeforms. He saw a squirrel change its course rapidly to go in his same direction when other animals usually went out of their way to avoid his presence. A flock of birds disturbed by his passing took off, only to fly toward him. And then he broke through into a clearing, and there it was, nestled among a dark grove of trees like a monstrously mawed cave fish, waiting to snatch anything that passed. A house, old and abandoned and menacing. But not really a house. A word from long ago, in a time he could barely remember, came back to him: *gardinel.* That's what this was—a gardinel.

He changed back to his man form, though he kept his acute animal nose and night-vision eyes. As he walked closer to the house, he could see the edge of the clearing was teeming with animals that had been brought to this place, but the sense of danger was so strong that the lure could pull them no further, could not override the desire to survive. For a moment, he thought he would be wise to avoid the house as well, but he kept going. Not only was he confident he could handle any danger, but now that he was this close, he could sense a kind of familiarity.

The house was bathed in shadow and caked with dirt and detritus. It looked as dead and uninhabited as any could be. And yet, as he ascended the porch steps, the man in the denim jacket felt it tremble with life and purpose. The signal coalesced into a low whisper, something even his heightened senses could barely pick up. The door was locked but easily gave way with minimum effort. Even in the thick darkness, he could see the empty dining room with its dusty table, upon which was the near-mummified corpse of a dog, its blood now long turned to rusty flakes coating the soiled tablecloth. The shattered windows were clogged with dead flies and beetles, and a few small birds had impaled themselves on some of the shards, like the victims of a shrike skewered on thorn bushes.

He saw the hallways littered with dead rats and squirrels and lizards, and even without the voice in his head that was now growing clearer, he knew what it was saying.

Not enough, not enough, need more, so hungry…

Soon he came to the basement door. It had been bolted with heavy locks that even with tarnished age held fast, and the barricade was further reinforced by stout oak boards hammered into place across the entrance. With time he could have bashed his way in, but instead the drifter closed his eyes and focused on pulling his body apart, scattering his cells, becoming lighter and less dense. Then he stepped toward the door, passing through its microscopic cracks until he emerged on the other side.

He floated over the broken stairs, which looked purposely dismantled with an ax, and solidified once he reached the concrete floor of the basement.

"Who are you?" a voice immediately spoke in his mind. It was as frail and raspy as a stack of onion skin paper.

The drifter let out a croaking sound before he found his voice, not from fear but because it had been such a long time since he last spoke. Months? Years? "I'm a friend."

In the center of the floor was a large patch of concrete that looked newer and had been poured hurriedly, leaving ripples in the surface like frozen waves. Carved into the concrete was a circle etched with complicated designs and shapes and words from a language he did not recognize. A length of rebar had been driven into the center of the circle.

"You spoke in my mind," he said. "Can you read my thoughts?"

"Once," the voice said. *"Yes, once I could have, easily. I could lay the most guarded mind bare, could rip out the deepest secret. But I'm too weak to do much at all now... It takes so much effort, but I have enough left to know what you are."*

The man in the denim jacket smiled. His mouth was crowded with needle-thin teeth. "I think you've been calling me here, waiting for someone like me. I think I'm here to help you."

The thing buried in the concrete, the thing with iron driven through its heart and its head bashed in by a sledgehammer, began to laugh. Its horrid noise sent the birds in the trees fleeing, but that was no matter. It no longer needed them.

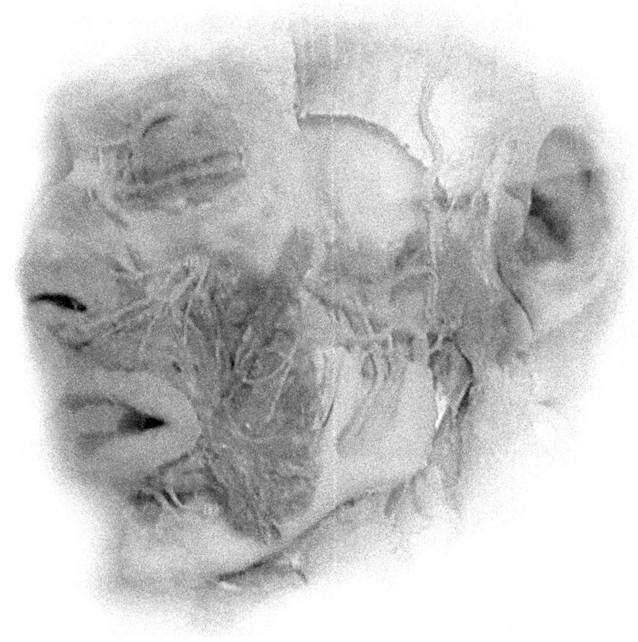

FIVE

The traveling woman knew she was being followed. Everywhere she went, no matter which darkened street she turned down, she could sense eyes on her. She didn't think she was being followed by one person in particular; if that had been true, she could have quickly spotted and dealt with them, perhaps by using her talents to squeeze their hearts to a pulp inside their chests. But there were so many eyes staring at her from under battered caps and out of dark doorways. Even the filthy pigeons and mangy cats seemed to be following her. Just to be safe, she had even displaced herself a few times. But within the hour, the feeling was back.

Perhaps the paranoia was well-earned. After all, she had been increasingly active these last few months. More so than usual for her, and that always brought undue attention. She couldn't say why she had been almost compelled to hunt more aggressively. It was as if she were preparing for something, building up her reserves of strength and power.

And how powerful indeed she had become with this increase in feeding. She could move multiple objects at once, manipulating them with a deftness she had never known before, or at least not in recent memory. She could reach down inside of someone and tinker with their bones and organs. Last month she'd made a man spend two hours watching his intestines be pulled out, using her power to staunch the bleeding and keep his synapses firing, feeding off such a well of pain and fear that she became bloated with it. She could jump further, more rapidly, and was less drained afterward. She'd used that to her advantage, one night committing two almost identical killings miles apart within minutes of each other. She supposed that passed as a joke for her, whatever sense of humor she had.

This flaunting of her power was unwise, though; she knew that. She had always been cautious and so very good at getting away. Showing off was so counter to her ingrained instincts it was like she was possessed. But for some reason, one she couldn't articulate, it felt *right.*

The traveling woman made three jumps in rapid succession, zigzagging across the city grid, popping in and out of space. After two hours without the watchful eyes resuming, she grew confident she had shaken what presence, real or imagined, had been around.

Now it was time for the true business of the night.

She could smell their fear and misery, hiding away under newspapers and squatting in derelict buildings, huddling to try to find some warmth against the night, or the demons of their own memories. She blended in with the people of the streets because she knew how well they were ignored. It worked to her advantage both as camouflage and as cover for victims. Seeming to be a filthy, weak little girl disarmed some, repelled others, and for those it attracted, like the sweaty man with the bayonet last week—people who thought they could victimize her—well, it was always easier when her prey walked right into her.

In the distance, sirens screamed, and people shouted in angry, unintelligible voices. The hazy night was broken by garish licks of neon and harsh billboards. The city seemed so fecund with noise and stench, and as much as she flickered in and out, she couldn't find a place that didn't reek of desperation and hate and the frantic mental flailing of thousands going slowly insane.

She walked the wet streets in new boots—pilfered from her would-be attacker—and as she passed a condemned tenement, the signal blazed out at her, a black psychic wail of someone waiting—practically begging—to meet their bogeyman. Sometimes she experienced that when she showed up. She was merely confirming what they wanted to believe all along—that her victims had been waiting their whole lives to see her, just so in that moment before she ripped the fear out of them, they could point their fingers at the universe and say, *"I told you so."*

She sensed the person on the second floor, somewhere toward the interior of the building. She sent herself there, making the jump in less than a blink. Turning down a few dark corridors, she spied a shape crouching under a blanket in the corner. It looked like a woman with long, scraggly hair, and though she seemed older, that might have just been the shadows and the hard living of the street. She made her way toward the woman, gliding just off the floor to give her that first jolt of fear. But instead of fright, a kind of satisfaction came from the huddled woman. Not the pessimistic satisfaction of some of her victims who gave themselves over to fate but that of a task accomplished.

And then she saw how the woman's smile twisted her face unnaturally and a ghostly light danced deep down in the pits of her eyes. Another soul buried deep inside, a soul that didn't belong to the shell in front of her.

"You've got a rider," she said flatly.

"Yes," the woman spoke, her voice pulled into a deeper, throat-straining register. "I've been looking for you."

The woman's first instinct was to kill the shell out of hand, just reach deep into her scrawny ribcage and stop her heart. But she fought down her twitch of murderous self-preservation and asked, "Who are you really?"

"Someone like you."

She scoffed. The traveling woman had met a few with strange, wild talents, but none like her. None who had forgotten the day they were born, who were no longer even sure they had ever been born at all.

"I too have the hunger," the derelict woman rumbled. "The need to devour. You're strong. Not like the others I've met from time to time. Some of them were little more than beasts."

"Flattery does nothing for me. I'm going to need you to make whatever point you have to make and then fuck off. I have things to do." She didn't really need to guess what the rider wanted, whatever glad-handing was presented. She knew what her honed instincts were telling her. She was a rival. This was the rider's territory, and though she had been here for some time, her antics over the last few months had obviously drawn their attention. And beings like her didn't do well with sharing.

"I want to meet you," the derelict woman said, then added with a smile, "in person. To propose a…negotiation of territory."

"I don't have any territory," the traveling woman snarled. "I'm just passing through."

"Making quite a show of it, though, aren't you, for one merely passing through? No, I think you are settling in. Which is why I'm proposing this little conference. Believe me, you should count yourself very lucky that I'm extending this courtesy."

"I'm sure courtesy is exactly what you have in mind," she snarled, and then turned to go.

The door behind her was closed, and ringing the exit was a hoard of black rats, extending three feet from the door and piled ankle deep, rolling across each other in a living tide. The room grew loud with their squeaking, and their doll-glass eyes peered out from bloated faces.

The woman spoke behind her. "I'm afraid the meeting isn't negotiable."

She spared a moment to look over her shoulder and bared her teeth at the woman before flicking out of the room, willing herself somewhere nearly two miles away. She popped back into space, suspended on a window ledge overlooking an alley, then floated down to the street. She was aware of a vague twinge deep inside her, something that might have been a human emotion like curiosity, or even shame. She didn't like having to run, but she was not inclined to face a mind pusher, especially one who seemed to be taking such an interest in her. Better to keep moving, always keep an eye out for trouble.

She walked on through the night, still hungry for a victim, but thrown off by her encounter with another who had a talent.

Perhaps tonight she would forgo her hunt after all. Maybe it was best to think about moving on. But that option rankled her. It might be the smart option, but it didn't seem *right.* What was this suddenly? This pride? This need to stay on some mysterious course that didn't seem her own?

Looking up at some of the people on the street, the woman noticed one of them, a bearded man standing on the corner, staring at her. That prickling sensation of caution began moving up her spine, and she had to resist the urge to make the jump right there in the street. Instead, she convinced herself that her warning system was still being overly sensitive and walked past the man, keeping her head down.

Just as she drew level to him, the man put a hand on her shoulder, and said, "I really must insist. You have my word, for what it's worth."

With the shock came the shove, almost reflexively. It wasn't a conscious, focused push, or the man might have ended up with a hole punched through his chest. Instead, the man toppled over and fell with a hard thwack against the building. The woman ran, rounding into the first blind alley she saw, and made another jump. She pushed herself further than she ever had before, and without even the idea of a destination in mind.

For a moment, she was surrounded by a howling void, and for the first time in as long as she could remember, she experienced true terror, thinking she had used her talent too much and condemned herself to some dark limbo where, being what she was, she would be denied even the eventual comfort of death. But then her vision was broken by pinpricks of light, and the howling became the merest murmur of crickets and nightbirds.

She was in a forest. Through a break in the trees, perhaps fifteen miles off, she saw the shapes of city buildings glowing faintly in the night. She laughed, both from relief and triumph. Not only because she had achieved her most ambitious jump, but because surely this was enough to throw her pursuer.

The woman heard a rustling in the tree nearest her, and she turned suddenly, this time making herself concentrate. She sent a strong, sharp barb of her power into the tree, sent it sniffing out life like a homing missile, and was rewarded when she heard the thud of something crashing to the forest floor.

When she walked to where the fall had happened, she first thought she had made a mistake. No body lay at her feet. But then she saw the glassy glint of recently dead eyes shining in the moonlight. Her grimy hands picked the creature up, brushing away the bits of leaves, and it took her a moment to recognize its odd, almost delicate form.

It was a bat.

Behind her the night exploded with flapping. The trees began to writhe with hundreds of bats, squeaking and flying in lazy circles. And though she couldn't speak to the animals, a part of her understood this display. She didn't know if she could credit herself with a flash of intuition, or if somehow the message was being conveyed to her through other means, but she knew her pursuer truly wanted her audience. And though there might be ulterior motives—of course there would be—none of them seemed to promise immediate danger.

"Okay," she said, dropping the dead bat. "I'll talk. Show me the way. But if you try and fuck me over, I swear I'll make you regret it."

The bats all rose from the trees in a single black tide, and the traveling woman bore herself aloft with her ability, floating above the treetops, flying with the bats, like a witch to a sabbath.

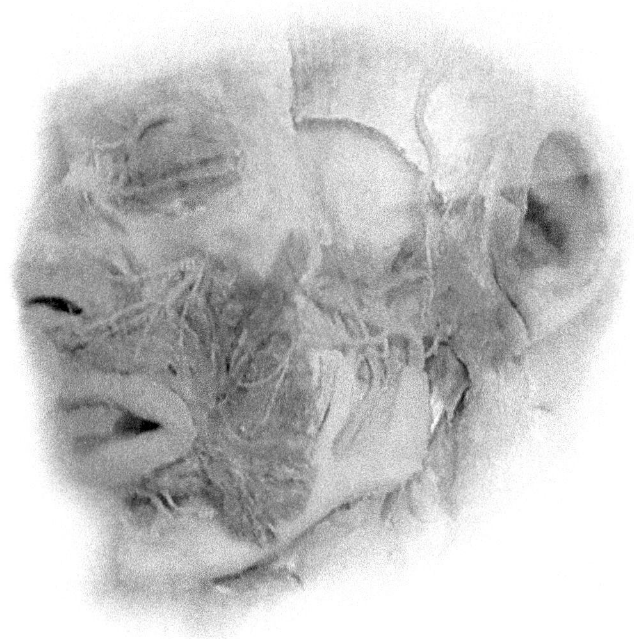

SIX

The thing in the basement didn't just need blood, like he did. It needed *everything*. He went out and caught a dog for it, scooping up the animal and bringing it within close range of the thing's influence. He'd offered to kill the creature himself and let its blood spill on the concrete circle, but the thing refused, saying it needed to exercise its abilities on larger prey than birds and rats. Likewise, the thing had turned down his offer to rip the floor out and free it, saying the process would be fatal in its current state of weakness.

Of course, the thing in the ground didn't say all this so much as it thought it at him. The man didn't know the full range of powers the thing would exhibit once it got out of its prison, but if it could speak telepathically and influence even small animals in the state it was in, then whatever mental powers it had were sure to be formidable. Coming quickly to this conclusion, the drifter was reluctant to continue his help. Who was to say that once freed, the thing wouldn't kill or eat him?

It heard his thoughts. *"Please don't worry that I'm planning on getting rid of you once I'm free. You are right to be wary, but I have had a lot of time to think here in the ground, and I have plans far beyond mere survival. I need someone of your strength and versatility to help with that plan."*

"And what exactly would that plan be?" he had asked.

"Later…" it whispered. *"I need… I need…"*

"I know," he said, letting his curiosity overtake his caution. Some part of him sensed this wasn't a trick, and he had hungered for a long time for some kind of change, some direction, a clear path to follow other than those dark, labyrinthine roads that wound through the night. He had longed for it without even being aware of what it was that he had wanted. But now, finally, there was a change.

So he'd gone out and found a dog—a plump, pampered Labrador he'd snatched out of a dark yard. The man had changed to something nasty and swift but still bipedal, so he could carry the dog. The animal's aggressive bark and ineffective bites soon devolved to pathetic, confused yelps as the man approached the house. Whatever weakened resistance the animal had been willing to put up, though, vanished as soon as he dumped it onto the front porch. It went silent and cocked up its ears, pawing at the ground.

The temperature of the air lowered, and the whole front of the house seemed to reek of a rotten miasma. He could see the shadows darken to an abysmal black, and he kept thinking he spotted movement from the corners of his eyes. He willed them to be multifaceted to try and get a better look, but nothing was there. Then he understood that there was nothing to actually see. The thing in the basement was projecting its essence up here to guide the animal downstairs.

The dog nosed its way through the crumbling door frame, ignoring the corpses of other animals and the putrescence the drifter, with his heightened senses, knew the animal must be aware of. What was the thing's astral projection doing to the animal? Was it casting some simple illusion, or pinching off a part of the dog's mind that made it sense fear? The animal followed an invisible path through the debris of gutted armchairs and the crashed chandelier, and not only was it not barking, but it was even wagging its tail. *Poor dumb bastard,* the man thought casually, but still followed, curious about what would happen next.

He had been at least allowed to rip open the door to the basement, thus giving the dog direct access to where the thing was buried. Previously, he had been told, no animal so ensnared was able to get so close, and so the thing was denied the full essence of even those meager creatures it managed to catch. But this time, matters would be different.

The Labrador bounded down the rickety remains of the stairs and leaped over the destroyed gap without hesitation, landing hard on the earthen floor. It went immediately to the corroded piece of rebar jutting from the concrete, circling it, sniffing and pawing.

Then, still wagging its tail, the dog began to bash its head against the concrete.

In less than a minute, it lay mercifully still, either dead or unconscious. The drifter then watched as the animal folded in upon itself. It was like watching something decay in accelerated time. Its skin tightened, its eyeballs withered, and soon it took on the pitiful, desiccated look of a mummy. He had seen some strange things. Hell, he himself was capable of strange things. But he was still taken aback at the rapid, brutal totality of the act.

"Yes," the thing said, and its voice in the drifter's mind sounded clearer and stronger, no longer frail and raspy. Despite the growl still in its sound, the voice had a vaguely androgynous, otherworldly quality.

The ground trembled beneath his feet. "Are you going to tell me now what this is all about? What you need me for?"

The voice sighed. *"You are special, like me. Each year, each wretched second, I've spent in this prison, I've sent out my beacon, trying to get someone like you to come."*

"So you just want to get out?"

"Of course, that. But so much more. There is another close by. I've read it in the minds of some of the animals I've taken, sensed that they've had their wills seized. So we have a pusher, a mind violator."

"Isn't that what you are?" the drifter asked. His abilities lay in the purely physical realm, and he had little understanding of the fine distinctions of mental talents.

"No," they said, *"I can touch minds, use the knowledge I've taken to manipulate and trick. I've convinced people to come to me by calling them in a voice they recognize, or made them see what isn't there. But I cannot force. I cannot invade. This one can. We need him."*

"For this plan you have?"

"Yes, and I will explain it all soon. But first…"

He raised a questioning brow in anticipation, knowing they would see the gesture, or at least sense the questioning pause in his mind.

"I'm ready to be removed from the concrete, though still much too weak for the binding stake to be taken out. There's a pickaxe in the corner. I'm sure you could make quick work of it."

The drifter started to get the tool, then paused. "I just want to be clear. I'm willing to help. Not because I give a damn about you, necessarily. But this is the first thing I've come across in a long time that could make me tell one night from the next. And I know I don't need to say this out loud, because you've got all your mind tricks, but I'll say it anyway."

"Yes?"

They seemed genuinely curious, and the man wondered if perhaps they could not read everything, after all. His voice felt strained and strange from all these words he was saying, more in these last days than in…what, years? But he was starting to get used to it, he thought. "I'm not your lackey. I'm not your follower. I know you're the thinker, and to you I'm probably not much better than some dumb animal, but I want in on this on the ground floor."

There was a pause before they said, *"I assure you, this is an…egalitarian endeavor."*

The drifter nodded, seemingly satisfied, then added, "Another thing: if you ever try to trick me, if you ever pull that shit on me like you did with this dog, I'll eat you."

There was another long silence, then the thing in the ground laughed like crumpled paper. It wasn't a laugh of derision, but of delight. *"I knew you were the right person for this job. And by the way, I'm not a 'thing.' I should like you to stop thinking of me like that. Call me…that word you called me earlier."*

He searched his memory of the conversation, which was enough.

"Thinker," they said, almost caressing the word. *"Call me Thinker."*

The drifter nodded again and swung the pickaxe into the cement. The explosion was tremendous, sending a shower of stone and dust. The implement vibrated violently in his hands, but his strength was true. He didn't know how far down he would have to go, but he didn't think it would take long.

"And you?" Thinker asked. *"What is your name?"*

He grunted. "Don't remember."

"I know," they said. *"You don't. The memory isn't there. Or it's so locked away even I can't find it. It's the same for all like us I've met. We always lose our names."*

"It doesn't matter," he said, swinging again in a mighty blow. The concrete was now mostly rubble.

"But it does. Names have power. The power to create or destroy. We need our names back."

The pickaxe handle broke. He tossed the rusted iron head aside and changed his hands into strong, clawed clubs, almost elephantine in their size, swiping at the ground in great blows.

"You are capable of amazing body manipulations," Thinker said. *"Usually those like you can only take on one alternate form, perhaps two. But your versatility, your ability to immediately adapt to whatever the situation calls for, is astonishing."*

The claws scraped against a coffin. Cocooning it were coils of iron chain. He snapped them apart, his hands now the scissors of a great crab, but he didn't open the lid. He would have to remove the rebar first, and he knew that now was not the time for that.

"You are Transmuter," they said with the authority of a priest at a baptism.

"If it suits you," he said, but underneath his laconic statement, he felt the stirring of something dark and powerful. And proud. "Now, how many people do you need me to kill before you can get out of this?"

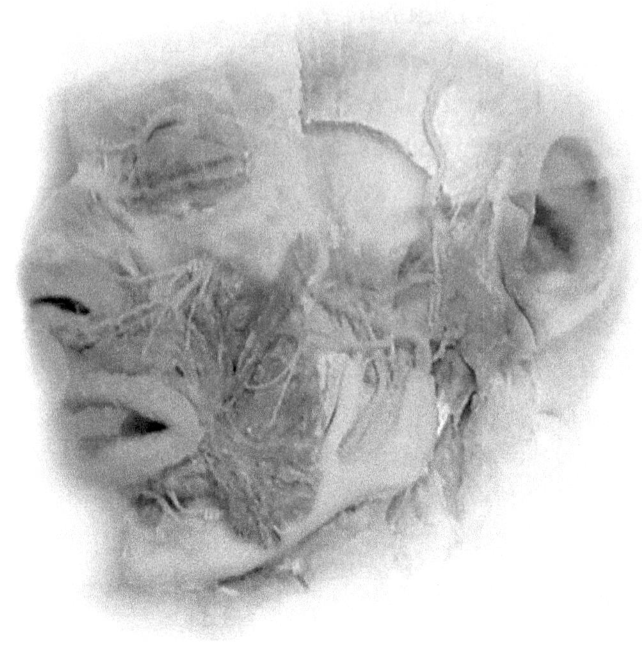

SEVEN

The dragon sat amidst his hoard, watching, touching, taking, talking. Always talking. He spent so many dark nights whispering to those upon whom he had given his mark, being the devil in their ears. Once he had touched someone's mind, however briefly, he could push them. Not very hard at first. That took time, more exposures to his influence and presence, more concentrated effort. But once he was in, he couldn't be expelled. There had been so many times when his voice was the little thing that finally pushed someone over the edge. His voice was the one that said to slap your wife across the mouth when she reprimanded you for drinking all night, to shake the shrieking baby, to turn a mugging into an impromptu mutilation. He couldn't claim credit for most of the misery that was around—people were quite capable of that all on their own—but he liked to think he had made a difference.

Sometimes, though, he didn't need to be so subtle. He had his loyal servants, whose minds he had reconfigured, who were all too willing to act as his proxies and bring him tributes. He thought he'd done them a favor. Most were so empty and lost when he'd found them. They were the kind of pliable fringe barnacles that drank poisoned sugar water or blew up subways. If it hadn't been him, it would have eventually been someone else. And really, wasn't what he asked for much less? When people were so willing to commit atrocities, why should they begrudge him his burnt offerings?

So he sat in his favorite chair among the glow of antique lamps, his ears deaf to the ticking of the multitude of clocks that adorned his walls. The stooped little man had entered a kind of fugue state as he did his rounds, checking in on his projects. In Bartlett Heights, an argument between a father and son spiraled out of control, and he made the father say that one more thing, that one irrevocable thing that always lurks under the surface of any bad fight—the one phrase that forever breaks a relationship. In the business district, he convinced a hard-drinking salary man, after his third failed promotion, two divorces, and two estranged daughters, that now would be a suitable time to take the little pearl-handled .32 in his desk and stick it in his mouth. Of course, he had been sure to guide the man's hand at an off angle, so that he'd make himself a broken-faced catatonic instead of a corpse.

After that, the man touched the minds of the helpers he had sent out that night on a very special errand, registering that they were approaching. He smiled, collapsing his awareness down to just himself, rising out of his chair.

The leathery whisper of bat wings against the front of his house told him the guest was here. He heard the creak of footsteps on the porch and walked to the door, anticipating a knock. But before he had even reached out his hand to grasp the doorknob, a rush of air struck his face and the woman was there. He had only a moment to process the twin emotions of anger that his house had been penetrated and impressed surprise at the woman's ability.

He'd known she could teleport when he used his proxies to track her, but it was another matter to see the display first-hand. The man had seen others move so fast they seemed to flicker in and out of vision, but he'd never seen one truly, instantaneously cross physical space and move through barriers. But he didn't have much of a chance to pay his compliments.

"I can pull whatever you have that passes for organs out of your mouth," she said in a raspy voice. "You shouldn't have followed me."

He held out a conciliatory hand, and said, "I don't doubt you could. You have quite a set of talents, which I've already been admiring from afar. But I have my skills as well, which you've already seen. I could turn whatever you have that passes for a brain into liquid, so let's not waste our time with threats."

"You hunted me," the woman reiterated, her mouth a snarl. "Nobody hunts me."

The man could feel cold tendrils beginning to search the lapels of his cardigan, as delicate as the feelers of an insect. He supposed it was an unconscious move on the woman's part. He was willing to give her the benefit of a doubt, because otherwise he would have felt obligated to kill her. Instead, he decided to placate her by doing what he did best: talking.

"I assure you; I mean you no harm. You're understandably cautious about my intentions. I've had very few mutually satisfying partnerships with others of our kind, as I'm sure you have, if at all. Normally, I'm as territorial as they come."

"Is this supposed to be reassuring?" she asked. The threat still loomed in her voice, but some sarcasm had crept in, too.

The man could now take in how she stood and how she looked. He'd noted the irrelevant physical characteristics from the eyes of his proxies, but here he could fully see and sense the tension charged in her every limb, the loaded-spring anticipation of every movement, as if she were constantly on the verge of teleporting. He suspected the telekinetic abilities were an extension of this as well, this need for proactive defense and distance. Already the man was sizing her up, getting a measure of her will.

"I merely say these things to be honest with you," he said.

"Tell me, then" the woman responded, "what's making this different?"

Instead of answering, the man pointed to another armchair. "Please, sit."

The woman glanced at the seat. "I prefer to stand."

The man shrugged and returned to his seat. The immediate danger had passed. If the woman had truly intended to kill him, she would have tried to do so by now. She was ready for his pitch. "As I said, I've been noticing your activity. The man you impaled on a 500-foot radio tower was my personal favorite."

"He was afraid of heights," she said in a quiet voice, and the man didn't think it was meant for him.

"While I admire your flair, your lack of caution left me perplexed. The mad ones, the drooling idiots, might go around leaving wolf bites on people, but we with some sense of self-preservation aren't so cavalier. I'm assuming you're not new to this?"

The woman hesitated before saying, "I don't know how far back I go. Time isn't right for me."

The man couldn't say anything to that. He could remember the passage of time much more clearly, if not in terms of years, then at least in distinct patterns of cause and effect. But though he knew he'd been at this a long time, long enough to remember when most people considered cars a novelty, his memory didn't go all the way back.

"Have you always conducted yourself like this?" he asked.

"No," she said flatly.

"Then why the change?" The man immediately read the response in her body language, which tightened even more, if that were possible. That was all the answer he needed. "You sense it, don't you? A change approaching. A preparation."

A cuckoo clock trilled on the wall, setting off a chorus of chimes and dings.

The woman's eyes darted to the group of clocks, and though her eyes stayed cautious, the corners of her mouth twitched. The movement had all the grace of a galvanized corpse. "What's all this junk you have everywhere?"

"Tributes. My clay jars of oil. My stone daggers and iron bangles."

The woman walked around the living room, taking in the candy dish of wedding rings twinkling with diamonds. He allowed her to use her powers to lift the lid of a cedar box, and he took relish in her raised eyebrow as she saw it was filled with dentures, glass eyes, and prosthetic limbs. The lid clanged shut, and her gaze drifted back to the dark hallways leading to the other parts of the house.

"Are all of your rooms like this?"

He waved a hand. "I have other requirements than just baubles, however precious they may be to some. Some sacrifices can only be made in blood. And pain."

She cocked her head, as if listening, then asked, "They aren't afraid?"

"Only if I require it. I prefer obedience."

The woman straightened up, and even in the glow of his lights, she seemed drenched in shadow. "Show me."

The man rose, taking a set of keys from his pocket. He led the way into the dim hall, noticing the woman made no footsteps behind him. He stopped two doors down on the left, unsnapping a heavy padlock that had been installed on the door. Even before he opened the door and she saw what was inside, he knew that the woman could smell it: the charnel house and the outhouse, an overwhelming olfactory tide of blood, feces, and decomposition. But if she was like him, she would sense more than that. Though in his house the scent of fear had been bludgeoned by the demands of fealty, it had been replaced by the creeping bouquet of madness. Minds had been shattered here. Spirits had been sucked dry like animal bones at a hyena feeding.

Only after the door had been opened could faint sounds from inside the room be heard, like a child's tuneless humming. She took in the tableau before her, expressing no shock or outrage that he could detect, at least externally. She was like him, then, dead to empathy, dead to anything more than hunger and restlessness. But what was that; did he detect her hand tighten ever so slightly on the door frame? Maybe she wasn't such a hard-case after all.

"How long have you been keeping these people in this room?" she asked.

"Two weeks," he said. "It took so little encouragement from me before they started in. I wasn't even the one to first suggest what they're doing now."

"How many were there to start?" she asked. "It's hard to tell."

"Six. See the foot over there behind the table? You know, sometimes I check into their minds to see if they need another push, and there's nothing. No resistance, no guilt, no conscience. They pick up this kind of momentum, I suppose."

"What do you get out of it?" she asked. The three wraiths remaining in the room had turned toward them while they were talking, staring at them with their sunken eyes, their blood-crusted mouths moving in silent prayer.

"It's okay," he told them, as gentle as an indulgent father. "You can keep eating."

The three turned back to their meal.

"If they have no more resistance," she asked, "why do you have to lock the door?"

The man turned to look at her, and for a moment he felt his calm drop as if it had stepped over an unknown precipice. If it had lasted a moment longer, taken even a further second to rein it in, the man didn't know if he would have been able to stop himself from projecting his full will on her, coring her out and eating her soul from the inside. That is, if he was faster than her teleportation. Instead, he closed the door and, despite a momentary petty urge to leave the lock undone, clicked the padlock closed. He looked at her again, the violence in his eyes subdued for now.

"Is this the part where you say that you like my moxie?" she asked, one corner of her mouth twitching upward.

The man let the silence hang between them for several seconds before continuing, "You know something big is coming—a paradigm shift. The time's come now to stop bickering, stop squabbling over our little empires and consolidate our resources. There's a house in this town, out on the edge of the municipality. It's only come to my attention recently. I think it's been…cloaking itself until now. My scouts have brought back things they've seen there, things they don't understand. But *I* understand."

"And you want me to, what, check it out? Be a 'scout' for you?"

"For yourself, too. You have unique talents and defenses. Something is waking up in the house. I've sent my own men out for information, and they've turned up nothing useful."

What that had turned up wasn't just nothing, but a nothingness conspicuous in its totality. The records and newspapers had turned up nothing, not even so much as a land deed. He'd sent a proxy posing as a salesman to the nearest of what would qualify as neighbors and had him discreetly ask about the house. The people had looked at his man, all ignorant smiles, and either ignored the question completely or talked to him like an obtuse child whose nonsensical questions could only elicit mild amusement and consternation. He'd found the last woman so infuriatingly unhelpful with her condescension and apple-pie mannerisms that he'd jumped into her mind as his man was leaving and made her bash herself into unconsciousness on the doorframe.

He'd tried more direct methods, too. Tried sending his birds and rats and wild dogs to investigate, but something scrambled the signal, overloading their already simple brains. Then he'd sent one of his proxies, one of his oldest contacts, a person he'd traveled through and used up so much the man was practically catatonic when not being used as his surrogate.

And his proxy had refused.

He wouldn't even step onto the wilted grass in the furthest corners of the house's yard. The man pushed with everything he had, but his proxy didn't so much as lift a foot. He knew he could make that foot lift if he took over completely, cleaned the man out and wore him like a diving suit, which would burn the proxy up, kill him within a day if he stayed or immediately when he withdrew his control. But if whatever was in that house could rebuff his hold on one of his subjects, he wasn't eager to expose himself to such a risk. For the same reason, the man refused to go there himself. Such direct action was not suited to his taste, in any case.

That night he made his recalcitrant subject eat a container of weed killer, and then he thought about his options. Just how many unknown factors would he be forced to deal with. There was at least one, the being that was going around pinning people to walls like butterflies and pulling out their ribcages through their navels. The one he'd mean to hunt down and kill. But maybe she could serve a purpose after all…

The man told her none of this, of course. He knew she didn't buy any of his grand partnership spiel anyway. He could turn on the charm all he wanted, but this one was too cautious, too savvy to be convinced that way, and if he tried even slightly to mind-mark her, she would bolt. He was hoping instead to appeal to her aggressive defensiveness, and perhaps her sense of curiosity. Something strange really was happening at that house—that he believed. And this looming larger change could have something to do with it.

He didn't have to tell her why he needed her. Yes, the ability to space-step was a selling point, but looking at her now, he could tell she knew why he needed her. Because she didn't ask why he didn't send a proxy, because she already knew he needed someone who didn't have to be pushed.

"Okay. I'm in," she said, and the man knew it didn't have a thing to do with her wanting to help him or being afraid or threatened or bowled over by him. And though knowing that made him want to crush her into a smear, he couldn't help but to admire it too.

He nodded. "Another thing. There's been people going

missing in the area. Not exactly an atypical thing, but I usually know the manner of these things. Not any of yours, I suppose?"

She shook her head.

"I have reason to believe these missing people have been taken, in one manner or another, by the house. I've been monitoring the area around the house and have seen things that point in this direction."

The woman smiled. At least the man thought it was supposed to pass for a smile. "You talk a lot but don't say very much, do you?"

The man only paused a second. "Something's been seen going in and out of the house."

"Not enough eyes to get a good look? 'Something' was the best they could do?"

"It changes. It flies, or runs on all fours, or turns to mist."

Her smile faded.

"Still in?" he asked wryly.

They had returned to the living room. The woman picked up a snow globe from the mantle. The globe housed a sleepy rural village, complete with grazing sheep. She shook it, watching the snow float lazily onto the thatched roofs.

She tossed the globe in his direction, and he caught it, holding it in his long-fingered hands with care.

"Want me to bring you back a souvenir?" she asked.

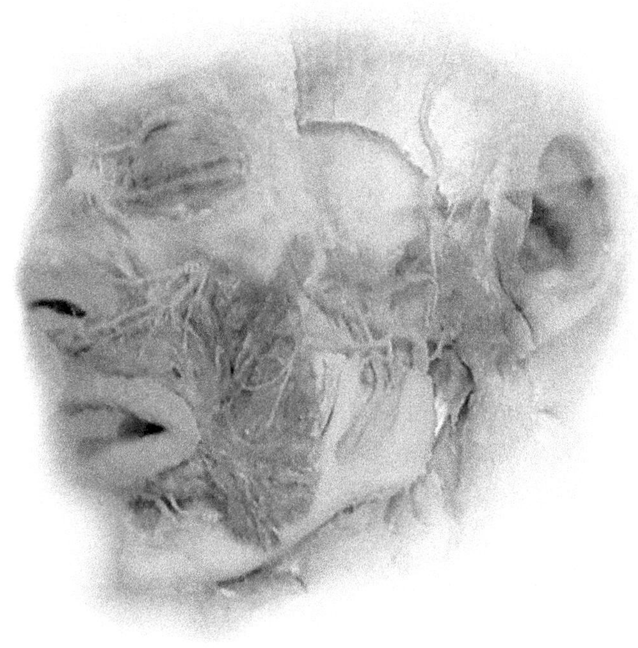

EIGHT

In a little less than two weeks, the changing man—
Transmuter—had fed six people into the house's dark heart.
Two others he had taken for his own needs. There had been
no strategy to whom he had decided to take, no concern
toward preying on merely the derelict and downtrodden like
some others did, not because he was incapable of cunning, but
because he couldn't be bothered to care. He knew such
guileless predation was his biggest weakness and that it kept
him always searching over his shoulder, always moving on.

He first took a pair of fishermen. Transmuter came off the
dark river in a cloying night fog, choking them unconscious by

gathering in their throats and lungs. Then he carried the none-too-light men back to the house, one slung over each shoulder. He didn't care for the extra work, knowing that if this had just been for himself, he would have taken both at the shore. But instead, he took them back to the house, down into the basement. He'd cleared away the concrete and piles of cold, gravel-encrusted dirt, digging around the rebar like he was uncovering a sunken monument. And per instructions, he had not removed the rod, nor had he tried to open the coffin lid.

"Do you need them to be awake?" he'd asked Thinker, laying the men on the basement floor.

"It's the most satisfying for me if some parts of their minds are engaged with me. I like to take everything, body and mind. But no, it's not necessary. Do you want them awake?"

"Yes," he said. "I want to see."

Transmuter de-corporealized into the basement wall so he could watch the men when they became conscious again. It wasn't like the dog, who had received a pleasant glamour, and even if it hadn't, the animal had no voice. But these men did.

As soon as they came to, Thinker assaulted them with horrific images. Transmuter only caught a few flashes errantly projected in his mind, but he saw enough to know the men were imagining each other as twisted monstrosities, things with too many teeth and amorphous, sucking limbs. One man beat the other to death with a spare chunk of concrete before tearing out his own eyes and bleeding to death on the ground.

When Transmuter next brought others to feed upon, the corpses of the two men resembled nothing so much as a pair of papery mummies. The time after that, they were brittle bones, looking as frail as chalk. And so it was with all that he brought to Thinker. He watched them all scream and swipe at imagined horrors that grew more complex and perverse as the thing in the ground gained power. He knew about mutability and altering himself in various monstrous forms, but in the end, he was limited to the raw mass of his own body. Thinker had no such restrictions, and they could immerse their victims in an entire world. He was shielded from most of the visions, but still those flashes crept through from sheer power: a river of moaning child corpses, a skinned dog shivering and snapping, a man's head collapsing into rancid jelly.

And finally, at the end of two weeks, the rebar was ready to come out.

Transmuter thought it would be like uprooting a tree, and he couldn't help but to think of a story he'd read somewhere about a boy pulling a sword from a stone. Then he caught himself wondering how that story had room in his mind, and how alien of a thought it was that he had ever done something as prosaic as reading. Had that been from before? And how long was it since he had even thought of such things?

"I can see so much now," Thinker said, the internal voice stronger, but still bearing that smooth, graceful quality. *"My net hasn't been so wide in so long. I'm so close. Pull the binding rod. And be careful."*

Transmuter braced his foot against the coffin, giving strength to his arms for the pull. But the metal slid out without resistance, making him stagger.

As he righted himself, the explosion came. The house seemed to shiver like an animal dying, and Transmuter could feel the dark energy rushing out, clutching at his fortress of a mind with clammy, insistent fingers. They were searching for any opening they could find, trying to pry open his head, exposing his thoughts like hot, quivering viscera. Transmuter could feel his body involuntarily shifting, trying to adapt to the psychic assault.

"Stop!" he growled, his jaw so distorted it could barely form the word. But his mind screamed it more clearly.

There was another discordant mental blast, before it clarified into a coherent voice. He could feel the pressure drop off suddenly, allowing him to get back to his feet.

"My apologies," the voice spoke in his mind. He could hear a faint babbling underneath it, like a tuneless chorus. *"What you just felt was not intentional. I'm perfectly in control now."*

Transmuter stared into the hole in the concrete. The coffin had blasted open, the rotted timber reduced to toothpicks. There was something down in the darkness, something amorphous and multilimbed that reminded him of nothing so much as a tree root. He knew he could adjust his eyes to see it better, but he avoided it instead, preferring not to.

"Where are you?" he asked, trying to not betray too much how on guard he was, the buds of extra eyes sprouting on the back of his head so he could see in every direction. But before Thinker even answered, he already knew, knew the reason he felt as if he'd been swallowed.

"Everywhere," Thinker spoke, laughter lurking in that mad, subaudible whine. *"Everywhere."*

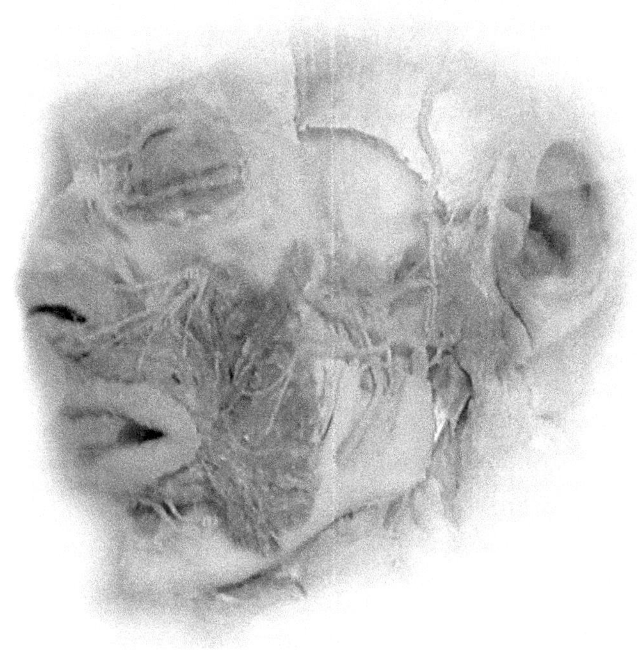

NINE

The traveling woman waited until the next full night to make the jump, since after her initial encounter with the mind-pushing man, most of that night was used up, and it would have been foolish to investigate then. She could tell he was annoyed with this delay, but she didn't really care. He could take her help or leave it. She was also smart enough not to make a jump too close to the house.

He had told her the address, and she had been somewhat startled to realize that she could not immediately place where it was. Her ability gave her a kind of innate understanding of geography, enabling her instinctively to know where she was and where she needed to go. She realized she would have to approximate the location, coming upon it tangentially. That didn't bother her; she would have taken this approach anyway. It was her lack of choice in the matter that disturbed her. She didn't like her hand being forced or her pathways cut off.

That was why she had come so close to killing the man who'd sent her on this task. When she had been confronted with his power, both through his proxies and in person, she knew that to engage him in direct conflict would be a dangerous undertaking, perhaps one that would result in her...death? She hesitated to use that word, since it implied that what she had now was life. If not death, then, the end of this existence.

If he had merely been a physical opponent, then she would have taken her chances. Her ability to instantly move through space gave her an advantage over the fastest of her kind, and her power of mind over matter meant strength was irrelevant. But the man's power to tinker with her mind had given her pause. Still, if he had truly threatened her, if he had tried to push orders into her, she would have attacked him, consequences be damned—him and as many catspaws he wanted to throw at her. But more importantly, the thing that stayed her hand was that she, like him, sensed the time was coming to put aside their differences and prepare for this change in the wind.

The traveling woman didn't know if exploring this mysterious house would end up being a help or a hindrance, but she felt that it was somehow a necessity. She was not inclined to philosophy or introspection—she had a feeling that was not uncommon among others like her—but with this rising change came that new awareness, that ability to plan, to think outside of the now. This new part of her considered the machinations of fate and felt inclined to dismiss them. With everything she had seen, with everything she herself could do, could she so easily rule it out?

She didn't like it at all. But the time for evasion was at an end.

The traveling woman made a jump within a couple of miles from the house. She ended up on the far outskirts of the city, and she was not completely surprised to find that she was near the place she had met her vespertilian escorts. The house was close; she could sense that now. But why had she not felt it when she was here before? It was an unmistakable—though subtle—sensation now, like the pull of the tides. Small, but relentless. She knew if she jumped without a destination in mind that she would instinctively move closer to the house.

So that's what she did, moving in hops not beyond her field of vision, no more than a few dozen yards at a time, before she could fix on a particular spot on the horizon. The geography clicked around like the shuttering of picture slides: cracked macadam under a bloated lemon moon, ramshackle houses with overgrown crabgrass lawns, a gutted dog in the ditch. She stopped at that last scene, not because the dog disturbed her, but because it only took her a couple of seconds to realize something was wrong with the dog's corpse. Though the dog was freshly dead, it had been untouched by any carrion eaters, as if it were so spoiled not even maggots would touch it. And it didn't take enhanced eyesight to see the enormous teeth marks that had ripped open its viscera.

She jumped again, following the increasingly strong pull, and suddenly, she was there, within sight of the house—even standing next to its rusted mailbox. Out of curiosity, the woman tried to read the name on the mailbox, but it had long ago weathered away. She had a feeling it didn't matter anyway, that whatever name used to be on this mailbox was merely window dressing—camouflage.

The woman chose to close the distance to the house on foot now instead of continuing to teleport, though she elected to use her ability to levitate slightly above the ground, gently parting the overgrown grass in her path. The house lay in front of her, and as the gloom cleared, she found herself shocked at its condition. The mind-pushing man had said the house had been abandoned for decades, but this house looked recently built, and of fine, even opulent, craftsmanship. The arched windows were dark, but even in the shadows, she could see the gaudy cupolas and porticos, the gleaming amaranth paint job. She wondered how anyone could overlook such an ostentatious house. But wasn't that why she was here?

As she moved closer, she thought she saw something moving in the distant trees. She whirled, sending out an instinctive mental bolt, the spear of force rattling the leaves of the copse of trees. Gathering herself, she thought perhaps she should rethink the frontal approach. The woman reached back into the woods, past the house's perimeter, and seized something alive, some wriggling rodent that pumped hot, fearful blood through its tiny body as it fought against the invisible force taking hold of it. She slowly moved the small creature toward the pink house, ignoring its panicked chirps that seemed so shrill in the quiet darkness. As the floating animal closed the last few yards, she saw a light come on in one of the upper windows, and a black shape unfurled from behind the highest spire. The shape swooped in on leathery wings, snatching the animal up and blurring back into the shadows.

The light in the upper window snapped off.

For a moment, she seriously considered turning around and walking away. Why should she have to go here? She had no obligation to do this and could see no clear gain from it, other than to perhaps better understand what was happening here. But no, she wouldn't be cowed. Let the house try to scare her off; she would shatter its precious arched windows and pull down its eaves. She could sense the power flowing through her now, stronger than ever. No, she wouldn't be scared off.

She mounted the front steps of the house, disappearing into the shadow of the sunken doorway, and extended her hand, ready to dismantle the door's locking mechanism. Before she could, the heavy oak doors parted on well-oiled hinges.

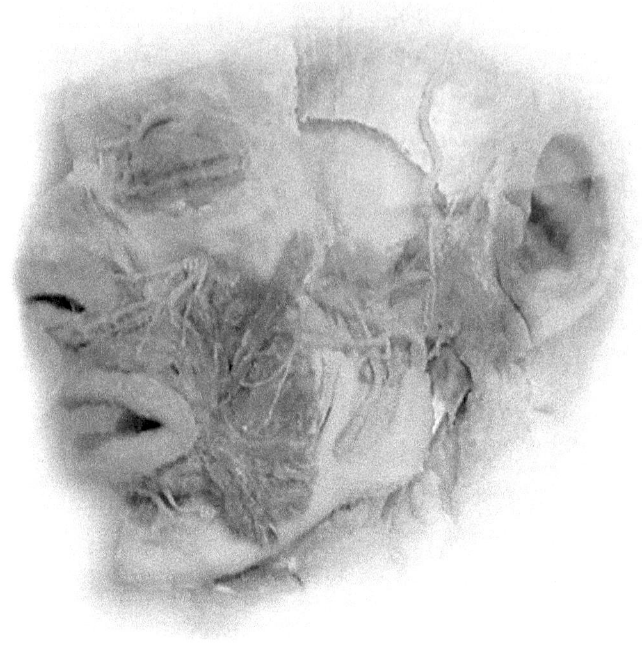

TEN

Thinker knew the woman was about to arrive. How could they not? They could see all, envision clearly in their mind the entirety of the countryside and the neighboring city. Thinker took it all in at once, reeling with the reclaimed power. It had been so long since they had tasted this glut of knowledge, decades since they had sat and gazed out in total awareness. Thinker saw the thousands of people crawling over each other like nothing so much as a mass of writhing maggots, and they knew that nothing much had changed. The clothes were different, and the people spent more time fiddling with their precious gadgets, but they were essentially the same. And that meant the people were still in need of Thinker's plan, of what they had been planning and turning over in their vast mind these many long years. It was the plan Thinker had been readying to advance the night they were first imprisoned.

Back then, they had owned the house instead of being a part of it. They'd had a form that passed for human, but Thinker felt no great mourning for that being in the past tense. Even then, they were trying for transcendence. They had tried to make others of their kind understand, and some had been starting to listen. They had slowly begun to consolidate their power, opened up to cooperation, and were willing to start playing the long game. But just as Thinker and their group were on the verge of moving forward in earnest, they watched as one after another of the potential allies were hunted down and dispatched. Thinker had seen their own executioners coming, and they could have run, but flush with the fervor of their upstart plans, they had decided to make a stand.

And Thinker had to give the hunting party this much: they had known Thinker was the strongest and most dangerous of the quarry. They'd come out in heavily armed numbers, adorned with their primitive amulets and not-so-primitive guns. Thinker had reached into their minds and pulled out their nightmares to use against them, and by the time they made it to the library where Thinker waited, only five of the original twenty had remained.

The entire magazine of a Browning Automatic Rifle and several rounds of 12-gauge buckshot had slowed Thinker down long enough for them to get the enchanted iron chains on. After that came a black absence, one even more pronounced than the vague amnesia their kind suffered from. When awareness returned, they had to begin from zero, building their powers and revising their plan. They found the flaws and strategized ways to get around them. And it started when Thinker revisited one of the most basic premises of the plan: why their kind existed in the first place. They understood now, and soon, they would make others understand. Though Transmuter did not comprehend some of the deeper philosophy behind the plan, he was on board, if only from a kind of relief from boredom. Thinker could work with that.

Now that the woman was closer, Thinker could truly sense her mind. A light touch was called for: their kind had chaotic, treacherous minds at best, and at worse, ones that could actively defend against any invasion or investigation. And of course, it was there, the madness and the memory, like rotten cloth. Be that as it may, though, Thinker saw the potential in her for true understanding, sensing not just an ally, but a collaborator. There was also the other man, the last of their quartet, the man who loved power and humiliation—the mind twister. He was an essential part of the plan, and now that Thinker knew more, both from the traveling woman's mind and their now greatly enhanced field of vision, the mind-pushing man would be the hardest to convince. But that was a matter for later; right now, the woman was here. And she must be tested.

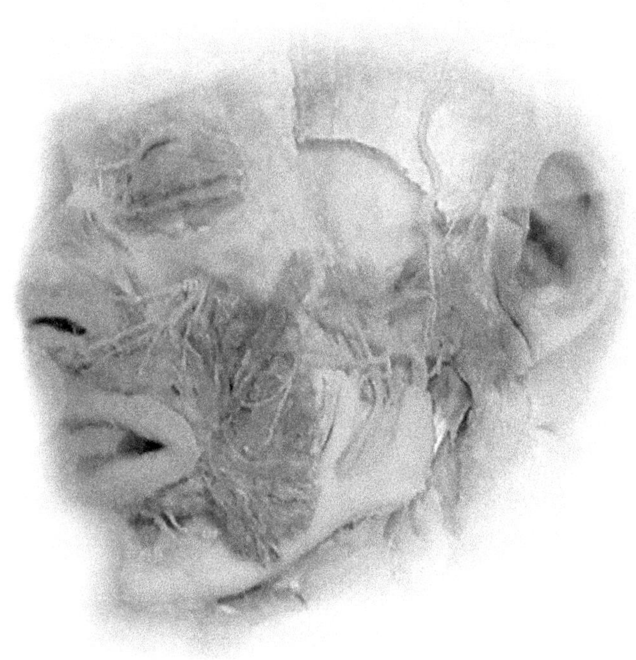

ELEVEN

At 17 Hibbing Street, the rats had come when beckoned, crawling out from among his prized bric-a-brac. A particularly large, vicious looking one that had once gnawed its own tail off to escape a trap scampered across the floor and came to rest at the toe of his master's suede loafer. The mind-pushing man held out his beringed hand, and the rodent leapt onto it, traversing the arm and coming to rest on his shoulder.

"Report," he stated, and the rat began to chitter, passing along the knowledge that had leapfrogged from one agent to the other. The woman had made it to the house, and she had gone inside. "And then?"

The rat's thought process got strained after that, as its meager mind tried to describe the thing that had gone into the house after her: a great beast with no form. Or many forms.

He frowned. Would his efforts be so easily thwarted? No, no, that's why he'd picked her. He didn't care how many shapes the house's guardian had, or how fast and powerful it was supposed to be; the woman could always vanish if she couldn't use her other ability to keep it at bay. Such a clever combination of tricks that one had.

The man caught himself, examined the strange emotion bubbling in the back of his mind. Was he just a little jealous of her powers?

Interrupting this novel sensation was another, one that he was more familiar with, but that no one had dared to level against him in quite several years. He was being watched.

He gently removed the rat from his shoulder and placed him on the top of the recliner.

"I know you're watching me," he spoke to his living room. "I can feel you trying to touch my mind. I would caution against that. You may not like what you find."

He'd always demonstrated considerable defenses against mental interference. Anyone who tried to plunge into his mind might find themselves sinking into waters deep and infested with nasty things. He felt the presence ease off, and as he smirked in satisfaction, a voice spoke close in his ear. *"I'll hold off from courtesy, not fear, so don't go congratulating yourself just yet."*

The mind-pushing man stiffened, readying himself to seize, to control and dominate. But he found himself seizing…nothing. Whatever had come to him, it was too ephemeral for him to dominate. In all his time, he'd never encountered anything quite like this, so he had never known this limitation to his abilities. Almost without thinking, he lashed out with a psychic shockwave of panic-laced frustration. His bloated rodent informant tumbled from its perch on the recliner, dead from an aneurysm.

"That won't work on me," the voice said with a hint of apology. *"I do hope your rat friend won't be too difficult to replace."*

By sheer force of will, the man reined in his emotions. He'd be damned if some voice on the breeze would disturb his iron self-control any further.

"Would you please be so kind," he grunted through blood-stained teeth, "as to grace me with your name?"

A gentle laugh tickled his ear, and the man forced himself not to flinch.

"So eloquent," it remarked. *"I've met some of our kind who have forgotten the gift of speech, but that doesn't seem to be a problem for you."*

The mind-pushing man managed a grim smile. "You're going to need more than flattery to make up for coming into my domain."

"I could say the same to you," the voice said, with no discernible malice.

As usual, curiosity, and an insatiable need to verbally spar, was starting to squelch the man's outrage. "So I'm speaking to one of the denizens of our mystery house?"

"You could say that."

"And I do believe I didn't catch your name."

The laugh again, the laugh that made the man think of dank madhouses, or perhaps some of the locked rooms of his own dwelling.

"I have no name, as you well know. None of us do. But you can call me Thinker."

He tossed the rat's corpse off the seat of his armchair and settled in. "How expressive of you. I imagine you are here to discuss the envoy I sent, since you knew to look here."

"I am. But I've been meaning to have this conversation with you for some time now."

The mind-pushing man's long fingers gripped the chair. He didn't care for being audience to anyone's court. "Do continue."

"You know a change is coming." It was not a question.

"Yes. I assumed you to be a substantial piece of that puzzle. Am I being told my reasoning was somewhat misdirected?"

"Not precisely. I am content this time to play the role of herald rather than mastermind. You've been around for some time, so tell me, are you familiar with hunting parties?"

Even if the voice had not given the phrase emphasis, he would have known what Thinker meant. He forced himself to release the grip on the armchair and drummed his fingers, trying his best to sound nonchalant. "I've heard of them from time to time. Little packs of yapping jackals. I have an army at my disposal. What need would I have to concern myself with them?"

"You and I both know there's a difference between a band of frightened miscreants and a proper hunting party. You

know they have talents, just like us. A hunting party is enough to overwhelm one of us singularly, but together—"

The mind-pushing man chuckled. "I don't need alliances, thank you. I am more than capable of keeping a firm grip on my affairs."

Thinker was undeterred. *"This isn't just about survival. It isn't about getting by in our little foxholes. It's time to introduce a new paradigm. And that new order involves all of us, including the scout you sent so disrespectfully into my presence."*

He sighed. "I suppose you'll be killing her now."

"Oh, not at all. Not at all. But she must be tested. There can be no weak links this time. Do you think she is worthy?"

The man smiled. "I'd be very interested to see how she handles your appointed guardian."

"Yes, we will see. And then perhaps we can talk some more. You're good at that, aren't you? A Talker."

He was thinking about this new world, a whole dark planet at his feet. "Ideas are only as good as the words you have with which to speak them, after all."

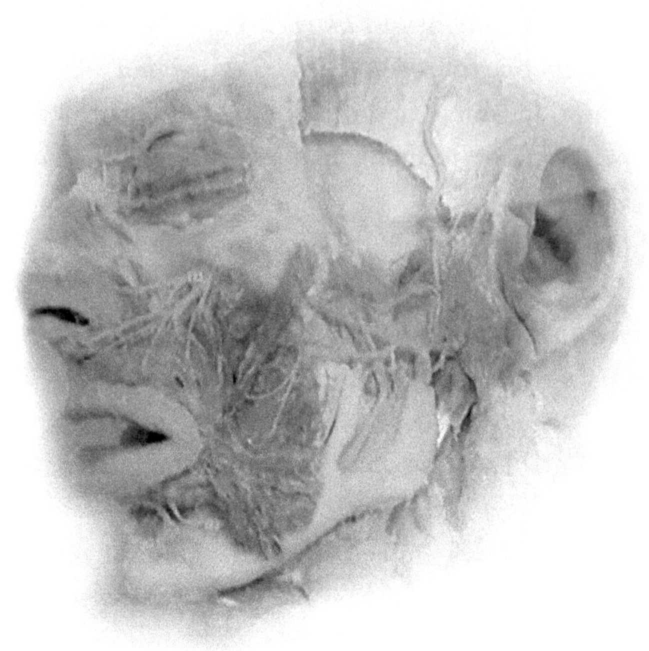

TWELVE

Transmuter curled himself around one of Thinker's cupolas, waiting for the right time. He'd briefly shown his flying form to the approaching figure, but it was all just a demonstration, both for the benefit of the would-be explorer and her sender. Such displays were against his nature. His shape-changing had always preferred function over form, pragmatism over psychological terror. If he needed to bite and render, he grew claws and teeth. If he needed to disappear, he dispersed himself enough to blow away into mist or step through barriers. He wasn't without his sense of the theatrical, apparently, for he did relish the terror that sat on the faces of his potential victims.

But what he was doing now was part of some game, just like he knew he wasn't really hiding behind some neo-Gothic protrusion, but merely squatting on the building's sagging roof. He was acutely aware of matter and forms, so he knew what his cells told him, even though he saw a sprawling rose-colored mansion. He could tell the woman in the yard could see it, too, because she had paused to take in the sight that wasn't really there.

Transmuter's preternatural eyes took in something unusual about her appearance: she never fully occupied any one space. The flickering was so quick that almost anyone, those with enhanced senses included, would have probably missed it. But not him. Here, like him, was another runner, another who had adapted for survival, for flight, for quick and aggressive defense. It made him feel a certain kinship with her, and perhaps a faint trace of guilt at what he was about to do. But it wasn't as if he was going to actually hurt her. He didn't follow orders with the zealotry of the converted, but he understood better than anyone what Thinker's plan was and what it meant. He knew how important it was, and it had indeed been a very long time since he had felt that about anything.

As the woman stepped onto the porch and headed toward the door, he dropped down from the roof, swinging on heavy, clawed, multi-jointed arms, and followed her inside.

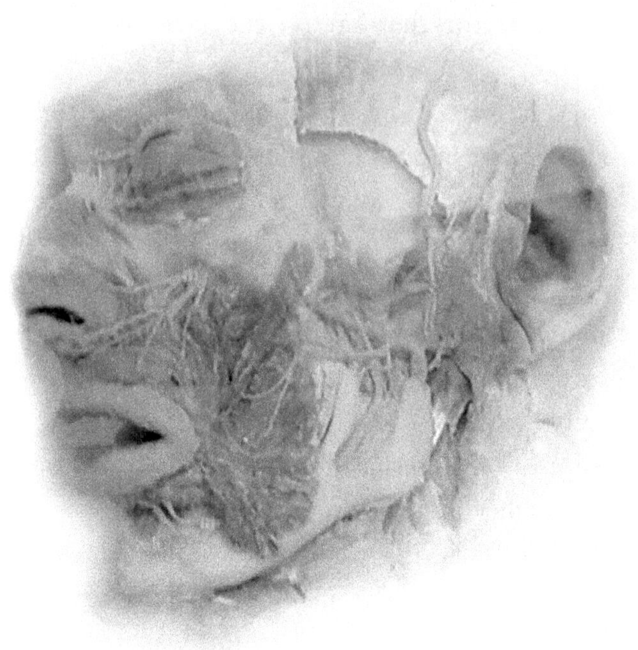

THIRTEEN

When she first entered the house, she could only make out the dark, amorphous lumps of what appeared to be furniture. As if on cue, lights flickered on from numerous decorative, gilded lamps, revealing an interior just as overdecorated as the exterior. The expansive parlor opened onto ribbed vaulted ceilings carved with dark wood, and rich tapestries adorned with heraldic images and Boschian hellscapes hung from walls papered with a faint fleur-de-lis design.

Her head sang with warnings to flee. Instead, she stepped further into the room, letting her feet come to rest on the lush, golden-hued rug in front of her. A staircase led into the dark interior of the house, and the woman thought the house was only revealing itself in pieces, that if she leapt into the dark space at the top of the stairs, she would not find more decorations, but something rotten. She drew in a deep sampling of the scents that surrounded her: wood, varnish, ash from the extinguished fire in the fireplace a hint of musk and mold. But if she pushed, there was another scent, like putrescent meat.

A tapestry of a maiden gently embracing a unicorn in her lap hung at the foot of the staircase. She reached out a small probe, just enough to ruffle the edges, but she did it with no advanced thought, snapping it off as instinctively as a blink. And though the tapestry did give a slow ripple, there was the slightest delay.

Thoughts of investigation quickly left her mind as a rush of air assaulted her from behind, the charge that always preceded an attack. Instead of turning, she made herself disappear, projecting herself closer to the doorway, where she presumed the new visitor was standing. This would put her at the physical advantage. And indeed, she found herself standing just inside the majestic doors of the house, firmly behind her would-be stalker. Except instead of looking at the back of a head, she found herself looking into two baleful eyes. He had turned to meet her. He had been waiting.

The figure in front of her bore the appearance of a tall, sinewy man with features that looked roughly hewed from wood. Long, tangled curls framed a stubbly face. The denim jacket he wore over a yellowed V-neck T-shirt was ripped and weather-worn, and the cuffs were stiff with dried blood. The same dark splatters dotted his twill trousers, making her think of house painting. His feet were bare and capped with thick nails that looked just as sharp as the ones on the end of his dirty fingers.

"The man with the animals sent you," he said, his voice croaky and tinged with an accent she couldn't place.

"I come for myself," she said, and supposed that wasn't exactly a lie.

The man's mouth rose slightly at one corner. "Looks like partnerships are new for you, too."

"Then you know what's going on with this house?" she asked. They had both started slowly circling each other, moving gradually so that they were now talking on either side of the parlor's claw-footed coffee table.

The woman saw a shudder run through the dirty man's body—not the kind of shiver resulting from the cold, but a kind of ripple.

"There'll be more time for talk after." Blood oozed from his mouth, dripping off his chin. When he opened his jaws, his teeth were like the edges of a ripsaw. The man moved so fast he seemed to blur, and the woman was sure she had seen him pass through the coffee table, as if it weren't there.

She didn't think to fight back with her telekinesis. She had just enough time, as the man's barbed claws closed around the lapels of her coat, to shift herself in space. Normally, if the threat were this severe, she would send herself far away, but instead she teleported precisely, placing herself above her attacker. She watched him grasp the empty air where she had just been, and he nearly stumbled. She almost laughed, but the giggle died in her throat as the man turned and immediately looked at where she was floating, as if he needed no time at all to spot her. Maybe he was like a shark, able to zero in on the field of her being.

Something twisted in the man's legs with a crunch, and he leaped toward her like a gigantic frog, his arms impossibly long. She waited until he had almost closed the distance and then shoved into him with her mind, swatting him with a vast mental fist. He catapulted through the air, crashing into the far wall and tearing down the mural of an armored man being knighted by a green-gowned woman. Underneath the tapestry the wall was stained, and the paint fell off in large pieces, exposing brittle wood.

That's the real house, she thought. *All this other stuff is a lie.*

The edges of the room blurred and then slowly rotated, attacking the woman's considerable resistance to vertigo. She teleported back to a standing position, trying to anchor herself as the room moved so that the left wall, the one with the stairs, now occupied the ground floor position. The stairwell yawned like an animal's gullet, and as if reading her thoughts, the rails to the banister snapped from their fixed positions and began flexing like numerous centipede legs. She thought she saw something wet and red down in that darkness at the end of the stairs, followed by a tremendous gulping noise, the sound a mindless hungry thing makes.

The woman closed her eyes, willing it away, knowing that if she fought hard enough, she could shake off the illusion. When she had met the mind manipulator, she had similarly not been afraid, approaching him with a kind of instinctual confidence. Perhaps the ability to manipulate physical force, to push others and herself, also made it easier for her to push away the encroachment of their minds. She concentrated, willing away the chimera, knowing that if she opened her eyes to take it in, or if she interacted with it physically, she would only strengthen the illusion.

Her surety was cut short by a tackling blow that lifted her off her feet. When she opened her eyes, she saw that the house had indeed changed. For one, the room had reoriented itself correctly. And though the house still displayed its neo-Gothic trappings, it was as if it had been dragged through decades of neglect. The colors had faded, the tapestries looked fungal, and cobwebs cocooned the furniture. Of course, she couldn't take much of it in, because the man in the denim jacket was upon her.

The skin on the tips of his fingers had sloughed off, exposing barbed talons of bone. His eyes grew larger, nearly bulbous enough to spill from his sockets, and his mouth split open as the skeletal, fanged muzzle of a wolf forced its way out of the ragged, bloody opening, snapping at her. The blood splattered her face, old and rancid, black like used motor oil. She stabbed out with a mental blade, keeping it precise this time instead of trying for a crushing blow. She heard the snap of breaking bone and then saw the back of the man's head explode, as if she'd just shot him with a bullet right in the fetid cavern of his mouth. He fell away, and she took the opportunity to teleport herself across the room. Surely such a blow would keep the creature down for a considerable time.

But she had only just regained her orientation when the man rose from the floor.

Another tactic was needed, obviously. The house was the true threat, the one capable of the greater power. She had to focus on finding the source of that power. The woman concentrated her power on the floor, seizing it with imaginary hands and ripping up a mass of wooden shards. She thought she heard a sort of high-frequency whine, like feedback. The woman hurtled the shards at the rising man, who was now beginning to sprout what looked like an enormous mouth in the center of his chest, its pink, wet tongue flopping and feeling its way along the dirty floor like a skinned snake. But instead of impaling him to the far wall, the shards passed right through him, as if he were as illusory as the other aspects of the house. He now oozed toward her, his body elongating and growing thin until some parts of it were almost translucent.

Rather than dwelling on the almost fascinating aspects of the man's transmutations, the woman investigated the hole she had just created. She could almost sense something down there in the darkness other than wood and insulation, something that made her imagine the word "orifice" or "wound" instead of "hole." A wave of revulsion fell over her, and then surprise that anything could make her balk. But she had no time now for hesitation, not with this shabby Proteus closing in. She focused on the orifice—*hole*—and space-stepped, only realizing at the last second that she had closed her eyes as tightly as a child about to descend the first hill on a rollercoaster.

A rollercoaster. Had she ever—

When she rematerialized, she felt entombed, as if she were in a cavity that exactly fit her body, but not an inch more. The woman heard a kind of mental vibration in her head, a tinny noise that sounded pained. She imagined her body wrapped in a sheath of pure force, and then she slowly inflated it, pushing it out against her skin-tight coffin. The woman opened her eyes, taking in the cavity she had created. With her sharp vision, she could see things moving and undulating in the darkness, seeping and blossoming against the telekinetic dome. She squeezed her eyes shut again, casting out with her innate sense of space, and jumped, hunting out the house's beating heart just like she'd sent her mind lance to find the bat in the tree.

When she reappeared, she was standing in a basement. It was an unremarkable space with rotten timbers supporting the ceiling above her, choked in the corner with dusty furniture and what looked like desiccated human remains. In the center of the basement's floor was a broken crater. A sickly *ignis fatuus* danced around the hole, suggesting shapes and images even more horrible than what she had seen moments earlier. But she believed she was seeing the house's true face now.

"I'm very pleased you found me," a voice spoke in her mind. *"You're even stronger than I anticipated."*

The voice was smooth and refined, as clear as one could be when there was no interference.

"No," she said, her voice steady, an icy resolve settling over her. "No more mind tricks. No more illusions. Don't use your talent on me anymore. If you have something to say to me, say it in your real voice."

For a moment, she was met with only silence, and she thought the house might retaliate with a monstrous illusion that would shatter even her abnormal mind. The woman gathered her strength, the cells in her body vibrating with power. Then she realized the vibration no longer came from her, but from the house itself. A phosphorescent glow hovered around the lip of the hole, growing denser, as if stuck in a gluey mass. She watched, almost hypnotized, as the weird fairy light began to pulse.

Then she saw movement out of the corner of her eye. She turned to face this new potential threat, and what she saw fascinated her. Her opponent from upstairs stepped out of the wall, as easily as if he had passed through a curtain. He would have looked like a ghost, except that once he came through the basement's wall, there was nothing intangible about him. Reluctantly, she prepared herself for another fight, but this notion quickly vanished when she saw the baffled expression on the man's face.

"What did you do?" he asked in genuine surprise, and she wasn't sure if the question was addressed to her or the entity in the floor.

When the woman turned back to the hole in the basement's floor, the light had settled like a glistening film over the hole and looked like nothing more than pale, clammy skin. The skin shuddered, and a puckered aperture blossomed in the middle. The floor groaned and buckled, and the air whistled around her. When the basement floor settled, she smelled a pungent blast of mold and carrion. It took her a moment to realize what had happened.

The house had taken a breath.

She imagined bladder-like sacs ballooning and withering under the house's foundation, moving the foul air in and out. And since the house did not need to breathe, just like her, it had to be taking in air for a different reason: to speak.

Despite what must have been the massive bellows of its ersatz lungs, the voice that drifted from the basement floor was thin and weak. "I hope…you take this…as a ges…ture of good…will." The gash in the floor moved with the words in an obscene parody of speaking. But she could understand it clearly enough.

"Goodwill?" she asked. "After you tried to kill me? After you sic your hound over there on me?"

The man in the denim jacket was at her side in one of his unsettling blurs. He looked angry but made no move to attack. "I'm no one's dog," he said in a flat voice. "Thinker and I are partners. I'm no one's damned dog."

She locked eyes with him and noticed one of his irises was a dilated blue and the other a cat's eye hazel. He demanded no apology, and she supplied none. But soon her mind was on another point.

"What did you say?" she asked. "Who's 'Thinker'?"

The man pointed at the grotesque opening on the floor.

"Thinker?" she repeated. "Is that supposed to be your name? We don't have those. We lost our names."

"Not…anymore," the awful voice in the ground said. The sound was so unnerving that she regretted asking it to manifest. It was gaining strength, sounding less tentative. "We will…no longer be bound…by the old roles. We will have purpose…and we will earn our…titles."

She turned to the dirty man at her side. "And do you have a name as well?"

"Transmuter," he said, with a sparkle of defiant pride.

"And what is this *purpose?*" she asked.

The membrane shuddered in the ground and drooped. "Transmuter will tell you everything. I can no longer maintain…this manifestation, and I will honor your wish to avoid…your mind. Though I hope that once…he and you have spoken, you will allow me to communicate with you…in the efficient manner to which I'm accustomed."

The woman thought it over for a moment, then slowly nodded. "Okay. I'll hear this plan. But one thing first."

"Yes?"

She hesitated for a moment, then said, "My name—it's Traveler."

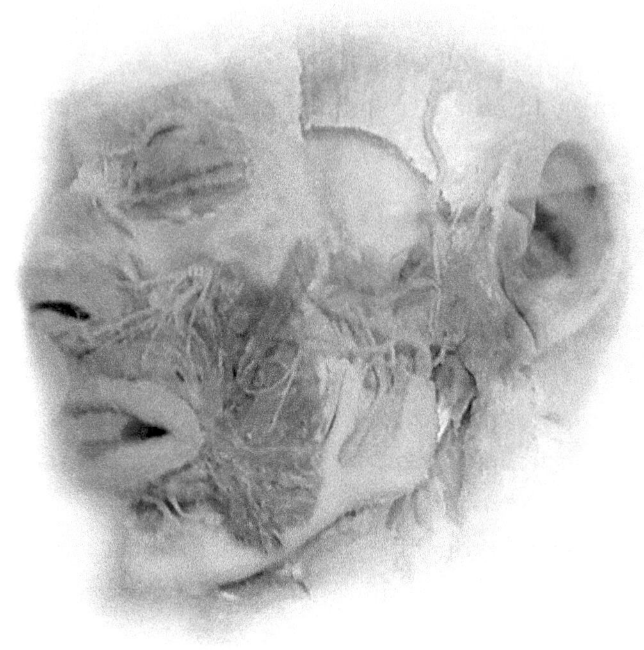

FOURTEEN

The parlor of the house was no longer the opulent Victorian monstrosity it had been when Transmuter had fought the teleporting woman, Thinker now having dropped the energy-exhausting illusion. Now the woman—Traveler—was liberated from the illusion as well, and so she saw the sitting room for the run-down, trashed hovel that it was. Though Thinker had told him that was of no concern, and that with time and energy, the house would start to repair itself.

He pointed to the sodden couch for Traveler to take a seat, and then wondered why such a gesture of courtesy would even occur to him. Indeed, why had he been the one given this task to explain the plan to Traveler, he who had almost forgotten how to speak? Transmuter imagined it was all part of the plan. His ability to articulate might leave something to be desired, but his level of concern over that fact stayed low. He would follow the plan, not as he had started—out of a kind of ennui— but because, as he slowly ruminated on it, the more it made sense. The more it seemed like the *only* course of action.

"Thank you, but I'll stand," Traveler said, and Transmuter found himself already thinking of her truly as such, as a part of the group, as if her cooperation were a foregone conclusion. Then again, why wouldn't it be? It was their destiny, after all.

Transmuter stared at her, silently wishing he had Thinker's ability to bypass the verbal and implant the idea into her mind, free from miscommunication. But such powers were out of his reach.

"I'm not good at words," he said. "Haven't had much use for them in a good long while. Just like you, I imagine. You don't trust mind tricks either, do you? So I'm going to tell this to you the best I can."

Traveler crossed her arms, and he heard the leather creak. "Seems like everyone around here has an agenda, except me."

"You mean your…patron? I can't say I know what his plan is, but what I *do* know is that Thinker has a role for him in our work. An important role."

Traveler smirked. "Is that so? I have to say, I've only officially met him the one time, but he didn't strike me as a team player."

"Thinker and he have spoken and come to an agreement."

She seemed taken aback at such a blunt resolution, but she

quickly regained her aplomb. "I don't know what kind of agreement they think they've reached, but I hope the two of you aren't naive enough to think he'll honor it. You think I walked out of his house believing I was anything to him other than a means to an end? I came here for me, and me only. To think otherwise is just asking for a knife in the back."

"We know," Transmuter said simply, trying not to feel insulted. "And I believed the same thing when I first met Thinker. It's default reasoning for our kind. Automatic, instinctual mistrust. It's that mistrust that's made us forget our purpose."

"Purpose? We don't have a purpose."

"Are you so sure of that?"

"Well, you can be sure the one who sent me here has a clear purpose. One he isn't going to compromise. I've met others like him before. They never do."

"His name is Talker."

"What?" she responded with confusion.

"The one who sent you here. He has a name now, too. *Talker.*"

"Did he come up with that one all by himself?" Traveler responded wryly.

Transmuter's own mouth curled slightly in bemusement. "In his mind he did, even if he wasn't aware of it. I'm sure you can agree it suits him."

Transmuter continued. "We know Talker is entering into the plan based on how he can best benefit. It has all been arranged. He plans to use the three of us as shields when the hunting party comes. By the time we have dealt with them, however, he will be in a better position to understand."

"Wait, a hunting party? What are you talking about?"

"Most normal people have forgotten us, or they like to pretend we don't exist. But hunting parties through the ages remember us. They know, and if one of us catches their attention, they will come. It's been that way so long that we've forgotten why we must hide. It's encoded in our DNA. Not all of us know the hunting party by name; we just know we run and hide. But now that's going to end."

"I don't see why we should be so worried with the talents we have," she said, knowing it couldn't be that simple.

"They have talents, too," he said. "Thinker isn't exactly sure to what extent, but they can't be underestimated. Just because we're going to stop them doesn't mean we can act like we've already won."

"So after we've dealt with this hunting party..." Traveler continued, trying to sound unfazed. "What next? This...plan?"

Transmuter nodded. "Have you ever thought about *why* we're here? Why we are the way we are, and what kind of purpose we're supposed to serve?"

She shook her head. "Why in the hell would I? I can't even remember how long I've been going on like this, or if there was anything different...before. Or if this is the way it's always been."

"Just like animals," he snarled, his face briefly contorting around the mouth, making it look as if his face were about to split apart. "No memory except learned impulses. No purpose other than rest and hunger and survival. I'm tired of being an animal."

Traveler looked down at her filthy rags and pilfered murderer's boots. She thought about the endless nights spent stalking the garbage heaps like a stray dog, of hiding in crawlspaces. It shocked her that she had never thought to ask herself that one simple question: why?

Transmuter saw the woman square her shoulders and knew they had her now, if not for collective reasons, then for personal ones. And just like with Talker, that was good enough for now.

"So what do you think our purpose is? To take over the world?" She smirked at that last sentence, and Transmuter returned the expression just like he had earlier. He wondered fleetingly if this was what charming someone was supposed to be like.

"No. No control. I think perhaps that was our mistake the first time. We are the servants, not the masters. We are here to guide the world to a better understanding."

"You've lost me," Traveler said, not with frustration but with the attitude of one who genuinely wanted to understand.

"People in the world now don't believe in the truly monstrous anymore. Oh, sure, they can see the monstrous in themselves, but I'm talking about them believing in evil outside of their own hearts. I don't mean some conceptual Satan that seems as far away as their God. I mean devils in the flesh, ones waiting in the dark places, ones as real as a mysterious breath on the back of your neck while you're sleeping. They don't see their world as an island in a dark sea. They believe that they are in control, that there is nothing beyond what they can see and manipulate. Granted, some believe, but those people are generally considered disturbed, or zealots. The world as a whole does not believe in something that is both otherworldly *and* tangible. They have forgotten the old fears that bound them together."

Transmuter was vaguely aware how foreign the words and ideas felt in his mouth, and he had an out-of-body moment—what others might have called a religious experience. His mind and body were changing, growing, adapting. Some dim part of him suspected his consciousness had been manipulated, that Thinker had slowly wormed their way in despite Transmuter's directives. Funny thing was, it didn't matter. He had never felt so charged with purpose or focus. If he were being manipulated, then he didn't want it to stop.

Traveler was quiet for what seemed like a long time, so long he thought he had failed. Then she said, "If they believe, they will hunt us even more. This hunting party won't be the last."

"Oh, of course there will be more. But if you think we will have entire armies raised against us, I don't think so. There will still be those who will deny, or who will shrink back from fear. But *enough* will believe, and they will see our forms in the darkness. And it will give us power enough to stand and fight and do what we must to achieve our purpose. It will unite us."

"Bogeymen," she said, the realization appearing to dawn on her. "We're supposed to be bogeymen." She said it with a hint of derision, then smiled, as if she had suddenly gotten the punchline of a joke. Her eyes caught the dim light like blades.

"Talker is the last of our group," he said. "Once we are all together, we can prepare."

Traveler turned to go, though she could just as easily have teleported away. Perhaps she thought it would be ill-mannered. As she was about to leave, Transmuter made a noise to get her attention. She turned to look over her shoulder, raising an inquisitive eyebrow.

He said, "You need to hurry. Thinker says the hunting party will be here soon, but they aren't sure where or when. They can't get a fix on the group, so they're guessing one of them is a dampener. That's someone who is immune to mental abilities."

She said, "Don't worry, I'll take care of it," and then she disappeared.

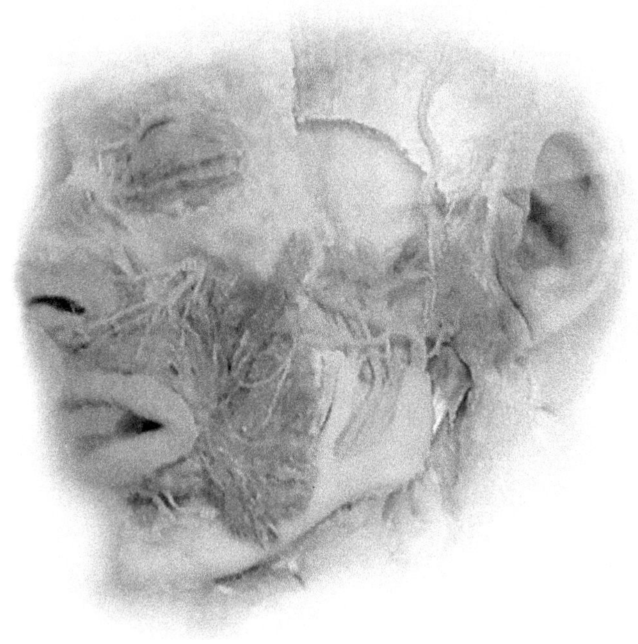

FIFTEEN

Talker. So that was to be his name.

He accepted the title with the kind of bemused graciousness one might give to a second-rate university bestowing an honorary doctorate. If, ahem, "Thinker" wanted to play their verbal games, then Talker was willing to indulge, so long as his own personal goals were furthered.

It wasn't that he found Thinker's agenda without merit. Quite the opposite. He could see the rationale in changing the rules of the game. Outsiders might view him as a sedentary hoarder, consolidating as much power as he could and refusing to shake the status quo if it meant jeopardizing his territory.

And Talker had to admit that was his mindset as of late. He had been content to let his proxies and agents do most of his legwork for him, and perhaps that had made him too complacent. He had lost his momentum and even some of his ambition. Here was an opportunity to regain his hunger, and if he played this correctly, if he bided his time, then maybe his gambit would pay off. He could turn the machinations of Thinker's plan to his own ends, and he had the advantage in that regard. Thinker was, in a strange way, an idealist. Thinker had a capital-P philosophy, and that would always make for blind spots.

It wasn't exactly that Talker underestimated Thinker, though. His encounter with Thinker was enough to convince him of the other's potency. Anyone who could astral project with such puissance, who was capable of such detailed and cunning illusions, would be dangerous to go against openly. It was best to go along for now and continue to pursue his own agenda. However, as skilled as Thinker was, Talker remained guarded against any potential attacks. As a mental manipulator himself, he understood how to block off portions of his mind, how to build traps and hidden rooms so expertly crafted that a mind scanner would be unaware they even existed. Thinker would therefore be blinded to his alternate schemes—though with their obvious intelligence, they would suspect him of ulterior motives.

But there was another reason he was glad he could wall off parts of his mind. The truth was he didn't need Thinker's silly title for an identity. Unlike others of his kind, he had not forgotten his name or his former life. His name had been

Stewart Mayhew, and though the memories of that life had grown hazy with the passage of time, it was also not a chasm. He could remember having a job, a home, even a family, though he was unclear of their names and exactly what the circumstances had been. He had been a teacher at an esteemed university, something related to history, and had collected first edition books and folios as a hobby.

He couldn't remember the events surrounding his…turning? The next clear memory he had was amassing his treasure in his first lair, the homeowner turned into a drooling psychopath in the attic that he occasionally fed people to. He had been a less deft hand at ensuring obedience back then: more of a butcher than a surgeon. The minds he had pushed then tended to shatter entirely.

Sometimes he would dimly wonder what happened to Stewart Mayhew's picturesque family. Had he murdered them all? Well, no matter. They'd be dead by now, anyway, and even if he had more details, enough to track them down and find out what really happened, he didn't care.

He was roused from his reverie by a fluttering at his window. A fat crow squatted on the windowsill, looking for a moment like it would tap on the glass. Talker sensed the crow had news for how things had gone at the house, though he suspected if they had gone that terribly, then he wouldn't have just had a peaceable conversation with the house's inhabitant. Thinker had told him the shield of menace had been reduced around the house, allowing Talker's proxies to go onto the premises without harm. He had immediately sent out a command through his mental network for those nearby to report to him.

Talker opened the window and held out his arm for the bird. The crow's talons dug into his arm, and Talker reached out to seize his information—and immediately sensed the mistake. Where previously there had been in the crow his complex directives and information caches, now there was something messy and organic and alien. The bird lunged at his face with astonishing speed, and though Talker's enhanced reflexes lashed out to catch the crow, his momentary confusion gave it just enough of an edge. Its ebony beak missed its presumed intended target—Talker's eye—and buried itself into his cheek, scraping against his bone. A faint, almost clinical, recognition of pain flickered across his mind.

It had been a long time since he felt anything worth labeling as pain. The most severely he had even been injured was on one of the rare instances he'd been caught sufficiently unaware. A group of town vigilantes had cornered him in retaliation for the cult he'd encouraged among the town's young and impressionable. They had cut out his tongue and severed his fingers before tarring and feathering him. The heat hurt worst of all, but he'd known if he didn't at least appear dead, they would set the torch to him. He wasn't sure if that would have killed him. From what little he had learned of his kind, it took more than purely human means to end them. But it likely would have put him in such a damaged state that it would have taken decades to recover.

Talker's hand closed around the bird, wrenching its beak clear of his cheek. The writhing crow raked its talon down, severing the end of his earlobe and leaving his cheek a gristly tatter hanging from the side of his head. With a vindictive sneer, Talker held the bird away from him and twisted its head off with a vicious grunt. Thoughtlessly, he stuffed the bird's squirting stump into his mouth, letting its dying pumps of meager blood drizzle into his throat, its wild tang lighting up his nerves. After a moment of consideration, he also tossed the crow's head between his jaws, crunching down, feeling its delicate skull disintegrate from his bites, tasting the slick ichor of its masticated brains and eyeballs. It was not his preferred sustenance, but it would encourage his wounds to heal.

He flung the crow's limp body away from him, cursing the bib of gore that now stained his shirt. He moved swiftly away from the window, correctly anticipating another attack. The window shattered, a bullet buzzing past his torn ear, punching a hole in the opposite wall. The impact knocked one of his prized urns to the floor where it cracked, spilling cakey yellow ashes in abstract patterns. Talker thought about what must be going on. He'd had his shelters attacked before, but not in a long time. He'd gotten comfortable here, entrenched, and had grown overly confident. It had been so long since he'd encountered a genuine hunting party that he had begun to believe their time was over, gone the way of witch trials and wolfsbane. But this had to be *the* hunting party Thinker had warned him of, the one coming in like a bad storm, otherwise they never would have been able to bypass his informants and get this close. Talker was taken aback and, yes, *offended* that the hunting party had managed to reverse the programming of one of his proxies. Sure, it was merely a bird, child's play to him, but it shouldn't have been possible for anyone else to turn against him. Talker realized that his cavalier confidence in the face of a potential threat, his dismissal of Thinker's warning, had been a dire mistake.

A handful of seconds had passed since the heavy caliber round had been fired, and with his heightened senses, he could already hear footsteps crossing his lawn. He didn't exactly live in the suburbs, but neither were his neighbors far enough away that they would be able to ignore a gunshot. Would this group be so brazen? No, he couldn't underestimate them. If they were cunning enough to take him on—and he would afford them cunning, if not intelligence—then they must have come up with some way to cloak the noise. He needed a plan, and fast.

His reflexes moving even faster than his thoughts, Talker was already sprinting toward the darkened inner hallway. He smiled, even though the movement furthered the rip in his cheek. His instincts steered him just where he needed to be. Yes, he still had some surprises for them. If they dared attack him, he would make them work for it. He would make them spill blood that wasn't his own.

He slithered along the pathways of his crowded living room with the agility of an adder, digging into the pocket of his khakis for his keys. He could still faintly hear the footsteps out on the lawn, moving cautiously toward the porch, though after such a loud opening salvo, he couldn't imagine the reason for their trepidation now. Grasping hold of the steel padlock, he twisted the key and yanked it open, quickly removing the heavy hunk of metal from the hasp and tossing it aside. He thrust open the door.

The stench of human misery and effluvia washed over him like a tangible force. Only two were left in his special room, and they had now lost all sense of humanity or morality. Lately, he had grown bored with them, and the hollow-eyed, emaciated, gore-encrusted wraiths no longer even acknowledged his presence. He had merely been waiting for them to die of infection or muster up enough shame to kill themselves. But now he was glad they had hung on this long.

"Rise," he commanded, seizing anew the strands of their broken wills.

Their psychic feedback was little more than white noise. The taller of the two had an untreated broken arm and an infected bite on his thigh, while the other man dropped some unrecognizable meat he had been chewing. Talker mentally instructed them to pick up the tools he had made available to them a few days ago that they had quickly abandoned in favor of bare hands. He effortlessly guided them, diverting fragments of his conscience so that they became like his extended limbs. The taller one picked up a razor-sharp boning knife while the other chose a rusty hatchet.

They shambled out of the room until he instructed them to get to the door more quickly. He retreated into the interior of the house, mentally planning his escape. It pained him to leave his shelter, and the thought of it made him feel like a turtle without its shell. But perhaps he could circle back later and reclaim his property. He had been so sure of his capabilities when speaking to Thinker, but now, with no idea of what abilities this hunting party had, he couldn't risk a head-on confrontation, not alone.

There was a back door near the kitchen, and he made his way toward it, while using his proxies to view what was going on in the front room. The one with the hatchet opened the front door and stood in the blackened frame. Talker had expected to see the hunters on his porch, hoping to take them by surprise. But he looked out at an empty lawn, the distant gleams of still lit windows far down the street and through a cluster of trees was all he could see. Then he noticed one of those glints was not a distant window but the reflection of light on glass.

His proxy's vision went out like an unplugged television, microseconds before another deafening rifle report echoed through the house. Almost by default, his vision went to his other proxy, just in time to see the one with the hatchet collapse to the floor, its head an obliterated lump of meat, brain, and bone. His remaining proxy pressed against the wall, hiding itself behind the open door. Within half a minute, he saw a rifle barrel appear in the gap between the door's edge and the wall.

Soon the entire person appeared—a tall, bulky man with a bristly brown crew-cut and wearing a gray-green peacoat. He held an enormous bolt-action rifle with a scope, a weapon that looked like it belonged on a safari killing elephants. This man rapidly scanned the room, then looked down at Talker's first proxy's corpse, seeming to realize only then that it wasn't his intended target. The hunter muttered a curse. While his eyes were downcast, Talker sent his proxy bursting out from behind the door, slashing out with the blade.

Without looking up, the man with the rifle flashed out his

hand, grabbing the knife from the proxy's weakened fist, ignoring the deep gash to the palm. The blade spun away, and seeing no other options, Talker broke his proxy's final hold on humanity, unleashing pure feral rage on the man.

It pounced, clawing with long, broken fingernails and snapping its blood-stained teeth. The sheer ferocity of the attack knocked the man off balance, but not off his feet. Where a normal man would have been beaten back by Talker's proxy, this man was incredibly strong. He delivered a knee to the proxy's gut, and though ineffective, it gave the man enough room to smash the rifle butt against its arm, breaking the limb.

The proxy attacked with its unbroken arm, but a new hand reached out and grabbed the arm. This person didn't have near the strength of the massive rifleman, but Talker found himself compelled to glance at the new threat, possibly forgoing the success of the attack. The woman appeared to be in her thirties, a head full of choppy blonde hair and a nose that had been severely broken at some point in the past.

"Stop," she said, and the proxy did.

Talker was so shocked that he almost lost his grip on the proxy but then realized his slipping control was not caused by his shock, but by a conscious and deliberate thwarting of his will. The woman somehow could affect his influence, and he suddenly understood she had been the one responsible for the crow's attack. He had heard of and even encountered those mortals who had strong enough force of will to withstand reprogramming—at least for a while. But never had he encountered anyone who could reverse his handiwork.

He pushed forward, trying to reassert his control over the

proxy, but the draining of his will was as inexorable as a severed artery sputtering on the ground. His remote vision through the proxy faded to a pinprick before disappearing completely. And then there he was, wholly back in his own body, huddled against the door to his kitchen. For the first time in a very long time, the weight of vulnerability settled over him like a cairn of stones. He had no physical prowess or skills over them beyond not succumbing to a normal death. He had to leave, and quickly, because he was no match for them without his mental abilities.

But he also quickly tamped down those feelings of weakness. He was retreating to assess and strategize, not running away. There would always be new empires to build. If he had been unwilling to lose a few choice battles, then he would not have survived this long. Once he discovered *their* weaknesses and how to exploit them, then they would suffer for infringing on his domain. He would turn their psyches inside out. He would debase them into inhuman animals, and they would call him Master before he made them eat their own tongues for being too unworthy to even speak to him.

He went to slip out the back door and had turned the knob when a noise gave him pause. It was a horrendous howl, the kind reserved for frozen woods and haunted castles. It had been quite some time since he had heard a cry of such unmitigated anguish, since those he victimized often did not have enough outrage to voice such a scream.

Talker perked up his ears, leaning into his heightened senses, to hear what came next.

"Jesus," said Rifleman, barely audible over the screaming. "This one is bad. Can't you fix him?"

"There's nothing left to fix," the woman with the broken nose said. "He's hollowed out. Nothing left but pain and motor instinct. Poor bastard."

A single pistol shot rang out in the house, and the screaming ended.

"Do you think he's still in the house?" Rifleman asked.

"Absolutely," she said, snapping the gun back into the holster. "He's a burrower. He won't run unless we flush him out. Little stoat."

Talker heard a zipper and some rumbling around, followed by the clatter of some of his mementos being cast to the ground. Then the woman said, "Hand me your lighter."

Fire. They were going to torch him. He knew now he had to run. Though fire was not the ultimate weapon against his kind, it would hurt him, and it resisted advanced healing. And if burned to ashes, he would have almost no chance of coming back, at least not in any form he cared much to inhabit.

He forced himself to push open the back door slowly and finish with his escape. He wouldn't ask Thinker or any of the others for help. He wouldn't have them see him being displaced. He knew he was outmatched here and now, but he would find a way without their false brotherhood. After all, if Thinker had warned him, if they knew the hunting party was on its way, where was the response? Could they not see what was going on? Could one of the members of the hunting party counter Thinker's all-seeing eye, just as the woman with the broken nose could undo his mark?

Perhaps it was a test, just like Thinker had tested Traveler. But he doubted that. Thinker was too eager to have him join them; leaving him to the mercy of hunters was not a way to win his support. Talker had to accept that maybe Thinker wanted to help, but couldn't, that their abilities had somehow been nullified.

Before stepping into the backyard, he not only checked it himself, but sent a report out to his proxies outside to let him know if the way was clear. He knew that until this threat was taken care of, he couldn't fully trust his extra eyes, not knowing if they had been compromised. Did the blonde woman only have the ability to reverse his influence, or could she infiltrate as well, going undetected in his proxies and secretly working against him? But until he had better evidence, he had no choice but to use what he had. And despite the doubts he harbored, the consensus among his animal scouts was that he would meet no resistance and that Rifleman and the blonde woman were at the front, getting ready to detonate their firebomb. So he stole across his back patio and slipped his feet onto the lush green lawn. Despite his losses, a smile crept across his damaged face. He had escaped against the odds once again.

He took a single step before he was shot in the chest.

Talker stumbled back against the railing of the patio, losing his footing, and went down hard on the final step, landing on his rear. He looked down at his chest and saw the white shirt quickly becoming engorged with blood from the raw cavity now above his heart. It must have just missed the organ, because if he had taken a shot directly to the heart, the results would have been catastrophic. A proper stake was required to effectively bind him, but a serious wound there made his kind so weak and vulnerable that it would be of no consequence to finish him.

Talker scanned his backyard in confusion, trying to see who had shot him, wondering how they had gone unseen. And suddenly the shooter was there in front of him, not popping into appearance as if he had been invisible but somehow stepping into his perception, as if he had been there all along. It was the same way dots that had previously gone unnoticed suddenly appeared with clarity in certain optical illusions, manifesting into a clear image, and it was hard to understand how you could have ever seen it any other way.

In fact, not just one but two people stood in front of him: a man and a woman. The woman's hand was on the man's shoulder, but Talker got a sense that this was not a gesture of comfort or affection. The woman's face was pulled into what looked like a permanent frown. Her forehead was deeply lined under graying hair, and her pale face floated moonlike over her black tactical vest zipped to the collar. The man was tall, and with his full red beard and tweed jacket, he looked almost professorial except for the large chrome .45-caliber automatic gripped in both hands.

"Got you, you son of a bitch," the red-headed man growled, taking a step toward him.

At that moment, Talker saw his darkened yard begin to lighten, dancing with orange illumination. More enraged than he had been in decades, Talker reached out with everything he had to attack the red-headed man's mind, prepared to rip it apart. But nothing happened. This wasn't like with the broken-nosed woman where his power had been countered. In this instance, there was no power there to seize *at all*. He was emptied.

"You just tried to mind-jack me, didn't you?" the red-haired man asked, and the gray-haired woman in the tactical vest left his side, walking over to Talker to deliver a swift boot to this side of his skull.

The heat from the fire grew in intensity, and he heard the crashing of wooden beams giving way.

"Let's stake him," the man who'd shot him said. "We need to hurry. He's not easy to nullify." He holstered the pistol and pulled out a small bag from his coat pocket, shaking a white substance on the ground. Talker recognized it as salt. The red-headed man was making a ritual circle around him.

Meanwhile, the woman in the black vest had drawn a massive Arkansas Toothpick dagger with an antler handle from a scabbard on her belt. She pushed Talker's head back, her creased face breaking into a smirk, and raised her arm to plunge the blade into his already wounded heart. But then, faintly, over the growing roar of the fire, Talker thought he heard an odd sound, one he'd only heard once before. By the time he placed it, the dagger disappeared from the woman's hand, wrenching her whole arm violently to the side. She cried out in surprise, and he watched her eyes follow the knife as it sailed into the darkness at the far side of the lawn.

Traveler had materialized in the yard. The harsh light of the fire showed the blotches of dried blood on her leather coat and the feverish blaze in her eyes. Talker could tell she had not been surprised by the scene. Either she had anticipated the attack—and if he survived this, he would have to find out how she found out *that* little nugget of information when he himself had been left in the dark—or she was so amped up that she was always ready for a fight, which was also possible. She planted her feet and both Talker's attacker and the red-headed man went sprawling like bowling pins. The woman in the black vest rapped her head painfully on the ground and seemed dazed, but the red-headed man quickly regained his footing. His salt circle stood as a "C" before scattering in a brief granular twister.

The red-headed man (whom Talker was starting to think of as Professor because of his tweed jacket) drew his chrome pistol and fired, but either he missed or Traveler had used her talent to deflect the bullet. She winked out and reappeared in front of Professor and from the smile that began to play at the corner of her mouth, Talker could tell she was ready to turn the man inside out. But then Talker felt his body filling back up with power, a vacuum broken, and he understood that Professor had lifted suppression from him. He immediately understood—the man could only neutralize one at a time—just as Traveler was assessing that she was now at a disadvantage.

To her credit, she adapted quickly. Talker watched confusion, shock, and rage flicker across her face within a second. As Professor leveled his .45 to shoot her in the face, Traveler reached out her hand as quick as a striking snake and manually shoved back the pistol's slide, ejecting the bullet in the chamber and jamming the weapon. The man had not expected her to regain her composure so swiftly, but he didn't have to worry long about suffering for underestimation. The other woman—Black Vest—had recovered and slashed out at Traveler with what looked like a kukri knife, opening a gash across her back, slicing through her heavy coat and opening her up to the bone of her spine. Traveler let out an enraged panther shriek, turning on her attacker.

Less than a minute had passed since Traveler first appeared, and even less since Professor had lifted his power from Talker. Even in his weakened state, his injuries were already healing, and his ability was coming back along with it. He would have preferred to seize Professor, but in his weakened state, Talker had to take the path of least resistance, and so he turned his power on Black Vest, whose mental prowess had been somewhat disoriented by the blow she had taken to the head. The invasion was not subtle, and the woman instantly recognized what was being done to her, screaming before her willpower was completely wrenched away.

Controlling Black Vest was difficult in his condition, and the woman lurched drunkenly toward Professor, brandishing the kukri, swinging it in wild, deadly arcs. Unfortunately, none connected, but the attack was enough to distract him from maintaining his suppression of Traveler, and she knew it. As Professor fought off Black Vest while trying to avoid injuring her, Traveler gathered her power, preparing to kill them both. Then Talker heard the booming report of the elephant gun.

Traveler didn't bother wasting time turning to see what the noise was. She instantly disappeared at the sound. She wasn't quick enough, however, and a fine mist of blood hovered in the air where she had stood. For a moment Talker wondered if she had taken the shot and would now be indefinitely lost in that strange in-between space she went to, drifting forever in a howling abyss. Talker turned to see Rifleman standing at the corner of his house, working the bolt of his weapon to eject the spent shell. He looked toward the now-empty lawn in confusion, advancing a few tentative steps. Talker wondered why he didn't come to the aid of the others, but then Broken Nose ran up from the yard's other side, tackling Black Vest.

Talker knew what was coming next and struggled to reorient his control to a new subject. Perhaps he could seize the giant marksman and gun all of them down. But as Broken Nose pushed his power away, Talker found that his well was dry again. He could no longer draw upon his own resources, and with the torching of his home, he had no reserve, no delicious symbols of pain and submission to feed from.

"It's okay," said Broken Nose to Black Vest. "He's gone."

Black Vest shook her head, as if warding off a swarm of gnats, and then she turned on him, her eyes hardening to rock. "We're finishing this now," she said, raising the kukri. "Screw the circle. We'll burn him after we take off the head. That'll be good enough for me."

"You know that—" Professor began, but Black Vest held up her hand. The quartet now closed in on him, with Rifleman bringing up the rear.

Talker could perhaps get to his feet now, but with the hunting party this close, he wondered at the futility of even trying to run. So this would be the end for him. It wasn't that he really thought he would end another way; he knew eventually his luck would run out. Honestly, he had never given much thought at all to his eventual end. Rather, he felt a disappointment that it was ending now, when the prospect of a new path had been opened by Thinker and Traveler, and new arenas to consolidate and increase his power.

The space between the rest of the group and Rifleman suddenly filled with a bloody apparition. The giant man actually flinched and almost lost his grip on the elephant gun. It was Traveler, with dark, black blood coating the left side of her jacket all the way to her wrist, where it had spilled out from the deep gash in her cheek that had been opened by that bullet moments earlier. Quickly regaining his footing, Rifleman went to raise the weapon to his shoulder, only to have its barrel sliced off by an unseen blade. He toppled back, shoved by a moving invisible wall, and Talker heard him grunt as his mouth and nose blooded. But Rifleman charged forward with renewed aggression, his mask of stoicism starting to break. Talker could tell Traveler was struggling to keep Rifleman at bay with her telekinesis.

Traveler turned back to the remaining trio. Black Vest was now back on her feet, and Talker focused on them just as she placed a hand on the shoulder of Professor and Broken Nose. They stood for a moment awash in the orange light of the flames shifting over them, shadows writhing among the glow. And then it was as if Talker's eyes slid off them. He knew where they should be, but suddenly they weren't.

"Oh, hell," Talker muttered, and struggled to his knees. Traveler was still fighting Rifleman, and though her power had opened painful-looking gashes, she hadn't been able to land a killing blow.

Talker gathered his strength and shouted, "They're coming!"

She turned at the noise, the distraction giving Rifleman the opening he needed. He seized Traveler's head in his tremendous hands, probably intent on twisting it off. Only when she found herself at this level of disadvantage did she finally teleport. The large man stumbled, with the pressure he was exerting now applied to empty air. He looked up, his feral eyes glinting in the firelight, before he too disappeared from view just like his companions.

Traveler reappeared next to him, the displacement of air making Talker's ears pop. He looked at her sunken, haunted face and noticed there a mixture of caution and pure exhilaration. He understood the thrill of struggle, but to take joy from direct combat was something he couldn't understand. Then again, she wasn't the one who had been shot near the heart.

She scanned the empty lawn, looking for any evidence of the hunting party. Once they attacked from the safety of their camouflage though, once a shot from Professor's pistol lit up the night or Black Vest sent a goddamn ninja star sailing through the air, Traveler would spot them and be able to zero in on the location, shielded or not. But the standoff couldn't go on much longer, and Talker could see her jaw set as she came to a decision. She flicked her hand out like she was swinging at a bug, and Talker heard the shuddering moan of torn timber, right before a flaming chunk of his house sailed over his head. The massive piece of gutter and roof crashed into the yard with an echoing boom, sending a shrapnel cloud of burning splinters through the air. He heard the sweet burst of cursing and grunts, and he saw Professor's sleeve appear as if behind a curtain, its cuff licked by flame, before disappearing again.

"Let's go," Traveler said, grabbing him under the arms as if to pick him up.

And then the world turned inside out. It happened so fast that he almost couldn't grasp it, but he spent most of his time in the interior landscape of the mind, and he could rapidly process information. It was as if the world had been folded into a tiny square and then snapped back to full size in a matter of nanoseconds. When reality smoothed itself back out, they were no longer in his backyard, but a dark garbage-strewn alley, and the heat had been replaced by the slushy drizzle of a coming storm. It was raining in the city. Traveler lost his equilibrium and went down on one knee. He heard a sound behind him he thought was the gurgling of gutters, then he realized that it was Traveler. She was laughing.

"It worked," she said. "I can't believe it."

"What?" he asked, trying to get to his feet. His body was still healing from his wounds, but his skin pulled tight against his skull, but the effort was taking a toll. His skin felt tight and brittle against his skull, and he could see his skeletal fingers as he used what little strength he had to grab onto a nearby dumpster and pull himself up to a standing position. Traveler did not bother to lend him a hand, physically or telekinetically.

"I took you with me when I jumped. I didn't know for sure I could do that."

"You never tested it?" he said, somewhat surprised. It would have been one of the first boundaries he would have tested, had it been his ability.

"I've never had a need. And I was—afraid that doing it might mess something up. That I might not reappear."

They were silent for a moment while Traveler's elation eased back down.

"We need to get to Thinker," she said. "Let them know that the hunting party is here. So we can prepare."

Now it was Talker's turn to laugh. Traveler looked at him, confused, before he said, "Oh, come on. I didn't peg you as so naive. Do you think that little shit didn't already know? That this probably was one of their precious tests? We're being forged, not recruited. And I won't be tossed into anyone's crucible."

"Like the others you use?" a gruff voice spoke from the shadows.

Talker's head snapped to the side. The darkness rolled like a great storm cloud before thickening into the shape of a man. It was Transmuter. He was still in his bare feet but now he had lost his filthy shirt, leaving only his tattered denim jacket to cover his torso. A crooked smile broke out amidst his stubble, and his black eyes glinted.

He tossed an object down at Talker's feet. It was a medium-sized dog—a collie, perhaps—that was intact but obviously dead.

"I smothered him," he said. "To keep all the blood in. I was told you would be hungry." His smile split his face open like a ventriloquist's dummy, opening back all the way to the ears. "Go ahead. Eat up."

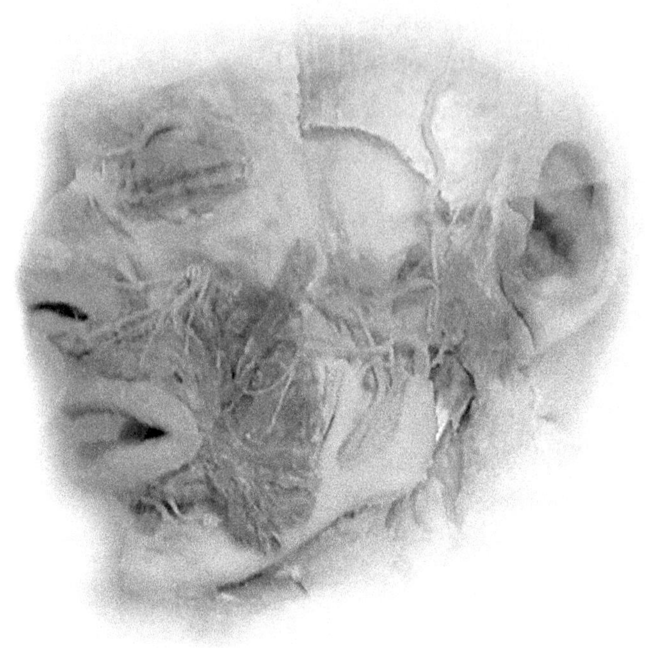

SIXTEEN

As soon as Traveler left the house, Thinker knew the first mistake had just been made. Not in letting her go to retrieve Talker, though that might appear to be the case. That silver-tongued packrat Talker was one of the wiliest of their kind Thinker had ever met, but with ones like him, deception was the expectation. No, the mistake was in thinking they still had a window of time to consolidate their power and focus their goal. And as soon as Traveler winked out of sight on the front porch, Thinker clearly saw the mistake. Because as soon as she did, Traveler disappeared from Thinker's mental map. She had entered a blind spot, and there could only be one reason for that. Thinker was surprised and frustrated they hadn't noticed Talker had already slipped from view, but the cloaking was not only there to block, but to make it invisible unless directly focused on.

After shedding nearly all pretense of corporeal form, Thinker had been able to magnify aspects of their talents to a heretofore unimagined degree. Though Thinker could no longer directly interact with the physical world, their ability to project their consciousness far away had increased vastly in range, to a surrounding one hundred miles, and was virtually omnipresent. Almost all minds were opened at a glance, with minimal effort. In fact, instead of struggling to batter down defenses to read the minds of the unwilling, Thinker now found the opposite was true: they had to close off the signals to prevent from getting overwhelmed. Illusions could be conjured with such ease and detail that they were only a step away from being able to manipulate reality instead of just the appearance of reality. And soon, with enough time and power, their reach might extend to a far greater area.

So there was no reason this absence would have gone unnoticed, not unless the person projecting it was powerful. With renewed determination, Thinker cast all focus toward Talker's house.

And the house wasn't there.

It was the most sophisticated cloaking Thinker had ever seen, and that fact alone brought with it the realization that not only had the timetable been wrong, but the power of the hunting party had been underestimated. Thinker knew firsthand that such a party should not be treated with anything other than caution. But they had not expected the hunting party to attack this fast, with this level of skill.

Since there was no way to check in on Talker, the assumption he might already be obliterated or otherwise beyond reach was not an unreasonable one. Thinker reached out to contact Transmuter, who was busy exploring and repairing the house. Before the thought could be fully formed, Transmuter was already standing at attention, dropping the armful of rotten wood he had been clearing.

"What is it?" he asked, his ears flattening against his skull. "What's happened?"

"I can't see the others. They're in a blank spot."

"What does that mean?"

The boards of the house creaked as Thinker involuntarily transmitted their pleasure. The man was so hungry for knowledge, for power. He was the perfect first ally. He was independent, but unlike Traveler, not a natural loner. He had his own initiative and would not be content as a mindless catspaw, but he would not make plans to hijack authority like Talker surely planned to. Transmuter's aptitude and powers could be utilized, and all the while he would be indebted to Thinker for the education he had been given. The applications of the man's abilities were truly astonishing, and he had only just now started to see his own potential.

"They are invisible to me," Thinker said, hoping Transmuter would draw his own conclusion, which of course, he did.

"Someone's putting up camouflage. No, not just someone... The hunting party."

"Yes. It appears we have been preempted."

"Then we should go out there," he said. "They won't be expecting all of us."

"No," Thinker said, gently. *"I'll be most powerful here. That is where we need to lure them. At this stage, we can't be sure how many there are. Traveler will be there by now, anyway, and I have a feeling she will be able to handle them long enough to escape and bring back details."*

"What about the other one?" he asked. "We need him if the plan is going forward. What if he's already dead?"

"We don't die easily. Even if Talker has already been attacked, even if the hunting party has started the killing ritual, there's a good chance she'll get there before they can finish. If anyone can find a way to get Talker out of that situation, it's her."

Transmuter nodded but didn't seem confident about it. Thinker had forgotten what it felt like to have to hold your ideas up to the harsh proving ground of reality, and they had to admit they had grown comfortable in their prison of concrete, that the hated tomb had become a shell where their grandiose plans could flow uninterrupted, with the logic and grace of a complex math equation. They had always been a cerebral creature, even when they had a body, but the decades spent frozen had made them forget how irrational and chaotic people could be, how so much could come down to sheer foolish luck. Through their twisting of the senses, Thinker had grown to see reality as something fluid that could be bent to their will. But despite being just as fluid as supposed, reality ran its own course—a raging, uncontrollable river.

Yes, Thinker mused internally, *but a river can be dammed.*

"Once Traveler gets out with Talker, we will rendezvous with them and prepare. Then we can be the ones on the attack."

Transmuter squatted on the ground, his legs twisting and his torso stretching so that he resembled a lean greyhound. Without needing another word of instruction, he bounded out the front door, leaving slimy paw prints in his wake. As Transmuter disappeared into the night, Thinker was so preoccupied with the shifting chessboard of their plans and how the hunting party would play into it that they almost missed something that had been unusual about Transmuter's departure. Though he had been in canine form and on all fours, he had managed to get through the front door, which now stood slightly ajar. Thinker had been looking at him when he left—though not truly observing—and he had not lifted himself up to open the door. Nor had he phased through it, because the door now hung ajar. Replaying the scene, Thinker saw what had happened: the door had opened by itself, as if an invisible presence had done it.

If they had a mouth, it would have been smiling. It had already begun.

Thinker let their disembodied presence float over to the open door. For all their powerful mental attributes, they had never in these years sealed in the ground been able to directly touch or move physical objects. It had been a massive effort of will to even take on the paltry physical form they had used to briefly communicate with Traveler. But now, Thinker imagined extending an arm out to touch the doorknob. They could feel the fine oak grain under their phantom hands and the autumn breeze against their invisible skin. They sent the power of their thoughts out through the nonexistent limb, bearing down with all their will to close the door.

The door didn't close. But, with the slightest creak, it moved. When Thinker withdrew their presence from the door, they momentarily caught the ghostly image of a handprint on the door's paneling, beaded with condensation.

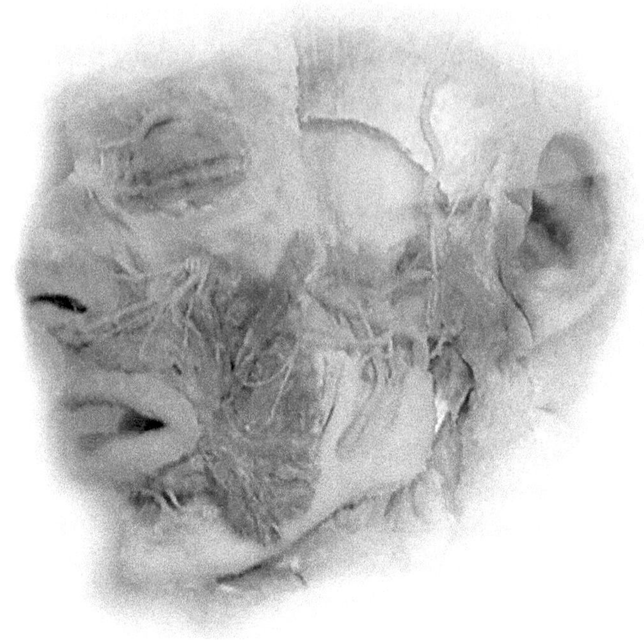

SEVENTEEN

The dead dog lay at their feet in the alley while they all stood staring at it, as if they were waiting for it to sit up from a prolonged trick. Transmuter's gaze moved between the two opposite him. It was the first time he had met Talker in person and the sight was not an impressive one. His shirt was torn open around his heart, stiff with black blood and pocked with black-ringed holes. A shard of wood was jammed into his upper right arm, and a large gash quivered on his forehead as it tried to knit itself closed. Transmuter could sense the work his body was trying to do to heal the broken bones and the wound so close to his heart. Talker smelled of burnt wood and blood and aborted magic, but most of all, he smelled like hunger. Transmuter knew that desperate need to consume, especially after being injured. Despite Talker's pretensions of civility, he was teeth and claws just like the rest of them.

"You expect me to use that?" Talker sneered, leaning against a garbage can.

"If you want to fight," Transmuter said. "If you want to survive. You know they'll come for us."

Traveler spoke, and though her words were directed at Talker, her eyes stayed on him. "He's right," she said. "You saw what they're capable of. We all need to be at full strength."

"We can't waste a drop," Transmuter said. Small orifices opened on the palms of his hands, long sandpaper tongues curling out of lamprey mouths, licking at the droplets of blood he had on his fingers.

Talker squatted next to the dog, groaning like the old man he looked to be. He opened his mouth to feed. Transmuter knew it wasn't his preferred sustenance, neither by method nor what his refined taste craved, but in this circumstance, it would have to do. Before biting into the dog, Talker looked up and gave him a baleful stare.

He made quick work of the dog, frantically feeding, ripping at it with his hands, cracking bone, and after a while, the alley was filled with nothing but wet, hungry, sucking sounds, not unlike a child nursing.

Traveler crossed the alley, giving the feeding a wide berth, and approached Transmuter. She too smelled of blood and flame, but much less so. She also gave off a palpable energy, but hers was not born out of desperation. Her shoulders were squared back, and her whole form seemed coiled in anticipation. But unlike before, when her tension was from paranoia and threat, she was now poised for action of a more ambitious nature. Transmuter had overheard her astonishment at her feat, at being able to transport more than just herself when she made her jump.

"Feels good, doesn't it —seeing what you're capable of, knowing just how much power is at your fingertips?" he asked her.

She seemed to ignore the comment, instead asking, "How much time do you think we have before they come after us?"

"Not much," he said. "I imagine they will regroup before the night is out. We have perhaps six or seven hours until dawn."

"Then we'll be vulnerable," she said.

"You know, I was thinking about that…" he began, before a voice cut him off.

"It's not enough," Talker said, his voice hoarse, his mouth smeared with blood. He looked frustrated, and dangerous. "The wounds have healed, but I'm not up to full strength. I can't see through my agents right now, though some of that might be because these hunting party bastards are disabling them. I need to re-establish control."

They both watched as he closed his eyes and began rocking back and forth on his heels, the orbs underneath his lids fluttering. His jerky movements and torn, blood-caked clothing made him look like a ghoul that had clawed its way out of a shallow grave. Transmuter reflected that there had surely been many times when he had looked just like that: feral and monstrous. And *mindless.* That was what bothered him most of all. He was still struggling to form strings of cause and effect that extended further than just a few nights. And he was casting his memory back through the past, attempting to trace some narrative in his existence, painfully piecing together a timeline that would lead him back to—what? His origin? His life before this? Could he even be sure there *was* a before, that he had ever been something else?

Talker's eyes flashed open, and before Transmuter and Traveler realized what was going on, he dashed out of the mouth of the alley. Given the early hour, and that they were also in the industrial part of town near the railroad tracks, there were no cars or pedestrians around to observe the blood-caked man and his two strange companions. Talker strode several yards to a nearby intersection and stood, like a man waiting for a bus.

"What's he—" Transmuter began, before seeing a glimmer of headlights in the distance. A vestigial instinct made him want to become incorporeal and fade into the ground to hide, but he fought back the urge. He had nothing to fear, and nothing to hide.

Even this most cursory twinge of caution proved to be unnecessary, though. As the vehicle neared, he could see it was a taxi. It first slowed, then swerved, its right front wheel jumping the curb and sending up sparks as its undercarriage scraped against the concrete. The car righted itself back onto the road before coming to a stop in front of them.

"I knew I could find one of them nearby," Talker said, walking up to the car. "I knew if I cast out my mind, I could find one of them close enough to obey, however weak I am right now."

The door of the taxi sprung open and a heavyset man with a green baseball cap stumbled out, reeling as if drunk. He completed the illusion by leaning over and vomiting in the street.

"I had to pull every string in him I had," Talker said. "No time for subtlety today. Not pretty, I know."

As Talker approached, the man straightened up to speak, and Transmuter could see the glassy, obsequious look in the driver's eyes, the mouth quivering and hands clasped together fawningly. Before he could utter his garbled stream of praise, Talker seized the man's head in both hands and slammed it hard against the side of the car. It met with a clang, and Transmuter saw the man's eyes flutter and then he fell unconscious, but Talker did not let him drop to the ground.

Pushing the driver's limp body against the hood, he bit down ravenously into the man's neck, working his head back and forth like a hyena at its prey. As Talker drank in the man's blood with gulping suckles, the taxi driver's legs spasmed, but soon grew still. Transmuter found it hard to tear his eyes away, both because he had not fed recently, but also because it was fascinating to see how quickly their kind could devolve. Was it possible for them to overcome this? How could they hope to plan and remember and have awareness when such desperate need was so close to the surface?

He turned to look at Traveler, who was also staring at the scene, albeit with a smirk. *She must be enjoying seeing him put in his place*, Transmuter thought.

Talker straightened, and Transmuter expected to see his shirt front drenched with blood even worse than when he had fed on the dog. But it seemed he had been careful not to let anything go to waste this time. The corpse at his feet was pale and slightly shriveled, looking like the desiccated bodies left by Thinker's first feeding. Talker used the tip of his long fingernail to scoop the single rivulet of blood off his face and licked it with a thin, probing tongue. He turned to face Transmuter.

"I want to talk to your boss, whoever the hell they are, and I mean now."

"Thinker is not my boss," Transmuter said flatly. "But we do have to all meet and speak together immediately." He turned to Traveler. "Do you think you can move all three of us back to the house?"

Traveler looked daunted at first, then found her resolve. "Yes, I think I can."

She stepped forward and placed a firm hand on Transmuter's shoulder, then she reached out for Talker's arm. He flinched and tried to pull away reflexively, but then allowed her hand on his shoulder. Traveler closed her eyes and took a deep breath, and before Transmuter could wonder if he should close his own eyes, the world winked out, and they were gone.

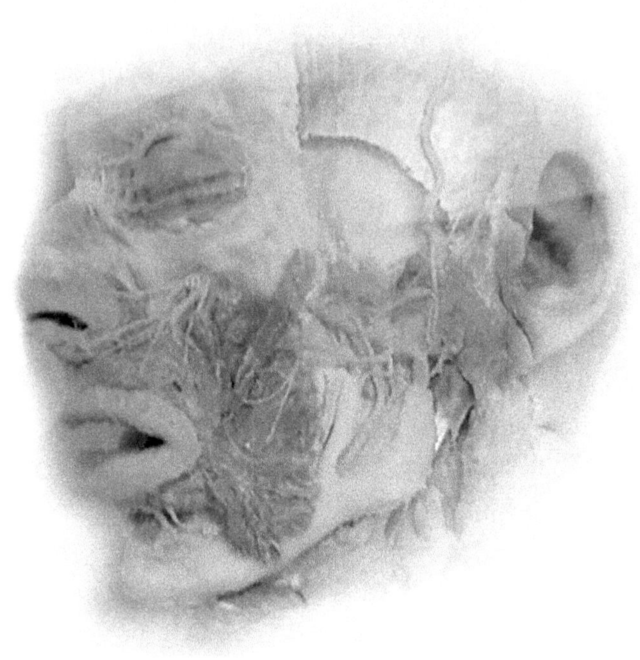

EIGHTEEN

Talker saw the world around him disappear, and he felt his body go weightless in the surrounding darkness. He had a momentary surge of panic, for here in the endless night was the thing that awaited in his nonexistent shadows, the part of himself that was more than him and from which he drew his power, the part of him too awful and alien to exist in this realm. And in that darkness, he was just a man, a tiny speck of nothing that the thing in the darkness would now grow bored with and cast off with the ease of a snake shedding its skin. But before that indescribable thing found him, the darkness ended.

No more than a millisecond had passed, but that feeling of

dread prevailed much longer. Instead of that endless, shambling nothingness, they all stood on the front lawn of an enormous house. Traveler stood on his left, and she let out a rattling wheeze of exhaustion. He glanced at Transmuter, searching his face as if trying to find any evidence that he had been shaken by what he saw. But his countenance remained as impassive as ever.

Once he had gotten over the jaunt, Talker took in the house before him. It no longer looked anything like the sagging, dilapidated hovel he had sent his scouts to investigate. Now it resembled a squat, gray castle, unimpressive but easy to defend. Its squared-off edges reminded him of a picture he had seen—recently?—in a book he'd been gifted, of Chillingham Castle in Northumberland. He wondered if Thinker was drawing specifically on that structure to create this utterly convincing illusion, which was perhaps almost as good as reality. But of course there was no way any structure like that could be rebuilt here in such little time.

What he did know was that the air crackled with power, the kind that had been charging when the hunting party readied to perform the killing ritual on him. It was the stink of magic. It didn't surprise him that so many of his agents had been killed or rebuffed trying to cross the threshold, and he was uncomfortably aware of being beyond that line himself, extended mercy from the house's defenses. He wondered how well it would hold back the hunting party.

"I'm glad you could all make it," said a voice in his head. He recognized it as Thinker's "voice," though it sounded fuller and more powerful. *"We have much to discuss before we*

engage with the hunting party, so please, invite yourselves in."

Transmuter dropped into an obedient trot, making his way across the lush green lawn that was most certainly part of the illusion.

As if she were the one who could read minds, Traveler stayed behind, turned to him, and said, "What do you see it as?"

"A castle," he answered, surprising himself that he had not even attempted guile. "You?"

"Me, too," she said. "Just wanted to check. I still don't know if I trust any of this."

"And why should we? But then again, I suppose we have no choice right now. We still don't know how many are in the hunting party, but you saw what four of them could do."

"Then time really is crucial," she said, then vanished. The air popped as the vacuum created by her body's absence filled up, and Talker saw her reappear in front of the house's wooden doors, where Transmuter waited.

Talker felt like the butt of a joke, and that made the darkness in him bristle. He had a sudden urge to reach into both of their minds and break them, until they were drooling cyphers who would gladly gouge out their own eyes before committing the sin of looking at him without his permission. Then he would incinerate this chameleon house, consequences and hunting party be damned.

"Those aren't very charitable thoughts," said Thinker, without much rancor.

Not missing a beat, Talker said, "Well, since we're in this together, we might as well all know where we stand." He strode quickly across the lawn, reaching the doors where the other two stood.

"Duly noted," Thinker replied, *"It's good to see you engaging with your honesty. Not something you've had a lot of practice with, even to yourself."*

"What is that supposed to mean?" he said, but his question went ignored as the doors swung open.

"I could have conjured up a manservant to greet you, I suppose," mused Thinker. *"I'm getting quite adept at mimicking sentient life. But I think we're beyond such unnecessary demonstrations."*

The doors opened into a sparse main area dominated by a large mahogany table that looked suited to conferences—or a cadre of knights, given the setting. A candelabra with dripping tallow candles hung over the table, and though the further walls were swallowed in darkness, Talker could make out tapestries illustrating scenes of battle. He couldn't make out every detail, but he saw enough on those expanses of warp and weft to know they depicted slaughters more than they did combat. Pikes skewered supplicating peasants, knights beheaded kneeling priests, and black-hooded executioners nailed screaming officials to crucifixes. Flames and piles of butchered bodies adorned blasted earth, and above it all, in the smoke-filled sky, something looked down with glowing, approving eyes.

Three chairs slid away from the table, and for a moment, acknowledging the illusion, Talker thought he would fall onto the floor. But he found himself sitting on an actual chair, feeling the grain of the wood under his hands, the smell of the guttering tallow and dust on the tapestries equally realistic. Again, he had to marvel at the detail. It was the most compelling illusion he'd ever seen cast, and he ruefully had to admit Thinker probably could have made good on the presentation of sentience. And if Thinker's control of observable reality was so skillful, why exactly were the three of them needed?

He almost expected to have his question answered, but it seemed Thinker's touch had been removed from his mind for the time being. At least as far as reading it was concerned. The voice in his head spoke again, though this time he presumed the other two heard it as well.

"You all know we have a hunting party in the area. Though they targeted Talker first, we must assume they know about all of us. I can only imagine they went after Talker because he was the most sedentary of us, not counting myself. Perhaps they did not feel up to the task of confronting me quite yet. But they are certainly aware now of Traveler, if they were not already. Both of you survived the encounter, thankfully. I apologize, Talker, for the loss of your domicile, but at least the incident provided us with an opportunity to assess the abilities of these hunting party members."

"What if there are more than just those four?" Traveler asked. "We can't account for what they might be able to do."

"I understand your point. However, it is useless to fret and plan for factors we have no way of knowing. We do know about these four, though. That's a small number for a hunting party, I'll grant you that, but these four seem particularly talented and experienced. They are well-armed, and I'll

venture that at least a couple of them have some sort of combat training. I was not able to observe the events directly because of the psychic shield one of them projected, but by accessing your memories and running them against what I already know about hunting parties, I think my conclusions are sound."

Talker unconsciously rubbed his temple, disturbed that his memories had been played back like reel-to-reel tapes without him even knowing it. Instead of commenting on that, he asked, "Okay, what do we know for sure they can do?"

"The younger woman—the one with the broken nose—can counteract the effects of your mind control, and she is seemingly impervious to it herself. The other woman in the group, the one in the black vest, seems to be able to make herself and others close to her invisible, both from normal and extrasensory perception. The red-headed man can nullify any of our talents when he is nearby, but based on what happened when Traveler showed up, he seems only capable of blocking one of us at a time. The only member of the hunting party who can't cancel out or block us is the large man with the rifle, who seems to have superlative strength and resilience to injury and pain. We will have to plan carefully and be unpredictable. And we have one other advantage, one I suspected but was not fully aware of until now."

The three of them exchanged glances, trying to read which the others might already know the answer. But like Talker, they all looked equally clueless, which aggrieved him instantly. He needed to gain the upper hand, somehow, in this situation. But for now, he listened.

"It has been something of a pet theory of mine, while trying

to plan our new age and formulate certain contingencies, that there might be specific boons to managing to get a group of us to work together consistently. Something that goes beyond the mere satisfaction of working toward a common goal."

They continued. *"I don't know why we not only avoid each other but actively hinder each other's progress. Why, I thought, should we, of all sentient beings, with all our power, unquestioningly hold back our fellow kind? Who should benefit from such an arrangement? Perhaps at some point a seed of destruction had been placed in our mental landscape, an "idea virus" if you will, that spread to all of us, to those who came after, that we must bicker, that we must have no ambition or pride, that we must not consolidate our power. So, the natural question that follows would be, why could us working together be such a dangerous thing?*

"Traveler, Transmuter, tell me: have either one of you noticed a change in your talents, or even your general mindset?"

Barely pausing, Transmuter answered, "Yes. I can think more clearly. Remember things better. I can feel the passage of time now, distinctly, instead of everything seeming like one long night."

"Speaking of a long night," Traveler said, "we don't have much time before sunrise, do we? I know the nights are longer now, but are we going to have time to deal with the hunting party? How can we be sure they won't just wait until we go dormant and burn the house down?"

"That's a good question," Thinker said. *"You see? You're drawing conclusions, thinking ahead, preparing. We weren't*

doing that before. And to answer your question, they will come after us. I can feel it. They want a challenge. And we are about to give them some prompting. Yes, the next few hours before dawn will be very busy for our new friends."

Without planning, Talker found himself adding to the conversation. "Your theory doesn't apply to me. I can remember things from day to day quite clearly. And I've had my plans and goals for some time now." Though he was surprised at himself for speaking, he felt a smug satisfaction at poking a hole in Thinker's little "theory."

It was Transmuter who answered, however. "Are you so sure of that? What exactly have you planned? What exactly have you accomplished, with all your hoarding?"

Talker sneered, and for a moment something physically shifted inside him, pulling at his bones. The sensation managed to take the sting out of his indignation, and it gave enough of a window for Thinker to continue, diffusing the conflict.

"The ultimate point, my friends, is not that our mental faculties have been enhanced, though they have. Nor is the point that our talents are becoming more potent. What's important is that I believe our power is increasing because we are, in essence, sharing the load. When one of us thinks, all of us are thinking. Traveler can now use her ability to make all of us teleport, not just her. And I can see what all of you can see, and in turn give that vision to the rest of you. What one sees or hears, so do we all. With that comes a sharing of our powers as well. The talent of one will be the talent of all."

After a few seconds of silence, Traveler said, "Are you saying we can use each other's talents?"

"In time, yes. Right now, we are perhaps only feeling the beginning flickers. As we grow and expand and bring others into the group, we will become a singular entity, uniting to create a force greater than any of us separately. But in time, even that will not be true, because each of us will reflect the whole, a microcosm of talents and powers. Do you see now what we have in our grasp?"

"Is this all just theory," asked Talker, "or do you have some proof of this?"

In response, the heavy table rose several inches off the floor, wobbling like a canoe at sea, and then slowly settled back down.

"What is this, a séance?" Talker sneered. "Are we going to get some mysterious knockings next? Besides, we all know the table's just one of your illusions. You could have dragons pour down the chimney, if you're as good as you say you are and wanted as much. Can you affect anything that's real?"

Something like a massive hand pushed Talker away from the table hard, moving him and his chair half a dozen feet across the floor with an abrasive screech. And the push was not just a pressure; it had texture to it, clammy and yielding but impossibly strong. For a moment, Talker imagined he could smell it, too—a stench of swamp or sewer, both rotten and fecund.

He sat there, stunned—not from the blow, but from the display. Then he found his voice again, as he always could. "How long have you been able to do that?"

Traveler stood up, exclaiming, "But I just met you!"

Thinker replied, *"To answer your question, Talker, not*

long. Traveler is correct that I haven't known her long personally, but her conflict with Transmuter in my area of influence, and her intense use of her talent here, must have sped up the process. I would have processed Transmuter's set of skills first, naturally, but since I have no traditional body, that is taking somewhat longer. Also, since I am in many ways now primarily raw consciousness, my theory is that I can adapt more quickly. But this should be some encouragement to you all."

"And how is all of this supposed to help us with the hunting party, if we aren't there yet?" said Talker. "They might be sitting around for a while, but it won't be long before they come for us again. I tried touching their minds. They're ironclad. Relentless and implacable. They won't stop coming, especially now that we've hurt them."

"True," Thinker said, *"and since they have one of their members cloaking them against clairvoyance, I cannot find them easily. However, there might be a way around that. A way you are particularly suited to help with."*

"What?" Talker retorted. "Planning on using me as bait again?"

Thinker didn't bother to address the accusation, leaving Talker to wonder how true it was. It certainly felt as if he'd been the goat tied to a tree, left out for the wolves, and he was reluctant to help any of them out of simple spite. But he couldn't deny that he stood a better chance with them than on his own.

Surprising even himself, he said, "Okay, what do you need?" If Thinker had a face, Talker was sure it would be smug.

"We can use your network," Thinker said. *"Your strength has mostly returned, so you should be able to reach out to those under your control and use them to triangulate the hunting party, the way you did with Traveler."*

"She could teleport, which made it tricky," Talker said. "But these bastards are invisible. My agents are physically normal. They won't be able to sense them any better than we can."

"They've got to let their guard down sometime," Transmuter added. "Even if it's just for a second. And they might assume that they're safer, that we are resting and recovering, especially since it's getting closer to daylight."

Talker looked around at the two sitting at the table with him, and he felt Thinker's unseen presence. They were all looking to him to make the next move. Here he finally was, in a position of true power, yet it was different this time. They didn't have the mindless obedience of his agents and victims. Nor the reluctant authority given to him because they wanted to strike a bargain. They turned to him with a look that said, *We are all in this together. We are depending on you.* It was something he hadn't felt in a long time. Or had he ever?

Perhaps as much to distract himself as to comply, Talker closed his eyes and cast himself into his network. And this time he did not just pull his power up with a select few, but in every man, woman, child, and animal he had touched long enough to establish a link. Some were barely aware of his presence and were not good for much more than living cameras. Some were almost totally in his possession, their only autonomy to feed themselves and breathe, spending their time when not in use by him in a semi-catatonic stupor. He saw through all their eyes, all at once, his considerable mind overflowing with the input. And in those he could bend, he sent out the message and the image of the four who had burned down his home:

Find them!

He didn't know how long it would take until later. He wasn't even aware enough of himself to note the passage of time, instead bringing in and synthesizing all the information rushing toward him, adjusting when necessary, sometimes many at once. And then…and then…

He had them.

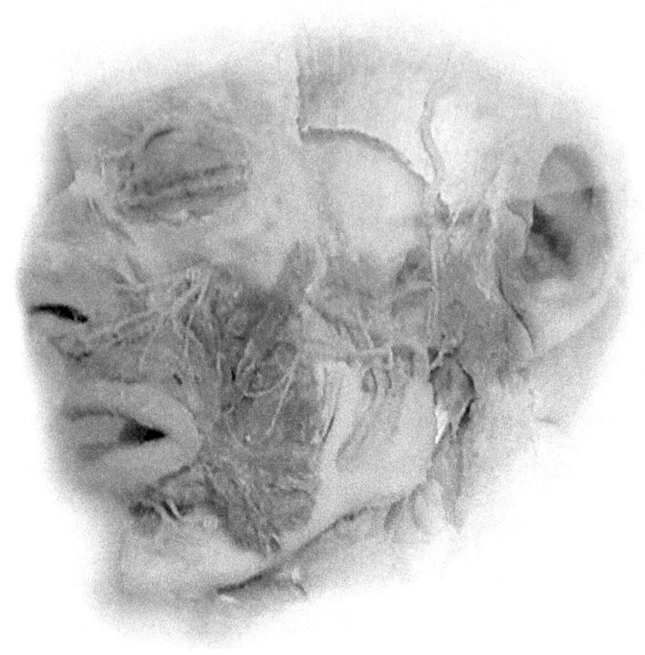

NINETEEN

Traveler sat across the table from Talker, watching him. He had been in a trance for nearly fifteen minutes without so much as an eye twitch to make him look like anything other than a corpse. His pallor appeared waxy and drained despite his recent feeding. She wondered what it must be like to be in that many heads, seeing through that many eyes all at once. Hearing all the howling and babbling that must be running through all their brains. It seemed overwhelming, and yet, if what Thinker said was true, there would come a time when she might control some inkling of this ability as well.

Of course, she remained skeptical of that theory. Even if it ended up being true, who knew how long it would take to reach even a fraction of Talker's ability? How many decades would it be before she could manipulate her flesh and bone the way Transmuter could? And conversely, despite Thinker's demonstration, perhaps it would take many years before they could wield her talents.

She had to admit, the thought gave her some comfort. She stopped for a moment to think why that was. Could it be that she was possessive of her talents? And if so, why should that be? Why should she care if Thinker could teleport the whole damned house off its foundations?

What bothered her was feeling like parts of her mind and her skills were merely tools, a wrench or hammer in someone else's toolbox. That's what was new to her: a sense of identity, an identifiable *me*. Just as she finally could identify a self, Thinker was talking about their personalities being subsumed and turned into an amalgam. Why should she immediately relinquish what she had so recently gained?

"You shouldn't think like that," a voice in her head spoke to her.

She jumped, still not quite used to Thinker's preferred method of communication.

"Don't think of it as a regression or a surrender of self," Thinker said. *"The plan isn't for us to just become a hive mind. The individual sense of self-worth, of accomplishment, is key. That was why the very first step was for us to regain our sense of autonomy, of being free from the shackles of habit, of unquestioning acceptance. Working toward a greater purpose as a group doesn't erase that."*

She crossed her arms and glanced around the room, wishing she could get a read on their face. "You just have all the answers, don't you? All the little explanations to soothe our doubts."

"I've had a lot of time to do nothing but plan for your reactions and questions, even though I didn't specifically know any of you yet."

"It makes me nervous when someone is too quick with answers. Most of the time, it means they haven't thought very much about the question. Or that it doesn't matter what your question was in the first place."

She looked over at Talker, still in his trance, but now starting to tremble and mutter under his breath. She looked at Transmuter, standing near the open doorway with his arms crossed, staring out into the night. Traveler got the impression Transmuter wasn't much for philosophizing. Yet, here he was, brow furrowed, his eyes bright with curiosity instead of hunger. What did he think of in those moments to himself? She knew Thinker and Talker had their vast, byzantine minds, but what did her and Transmuter have? What did they plan? What did they dream in those hours and years of sleep in the dark spaces that gave them refuge from the light?

Talker's jittering body snapped to attention as if jolted by an electric current, his long fingers gripping the arms of the chair tight enough to make the wood creak and start to splinter. His eyes rolled open, bloodshot and unfocused. For the flicker of a moment, she saw a picture in her mind as clearly as if she were seeing it in front of her: a dark building sandwiched among others in a dilapidated neighborhood. But no, not dark—a weak light in the bottom basement window. Then she realized how low the perspective was, not that of a person, but an animal. Traveler experienced a startling slide as her mind forked, taking in what she saw at Thinker's house as well as what she saw from the animal's point of view.

How does he do this without going completely insane?

With that thought, the fork closed, her attention returning solely to where her physical body was.

Transmuter had stepped away from the door. The look he'd had on his face, like an animal trying to understand a complex problem, had been swept away by a look of startled confusion.

"Did you see that, too?" he asked.

Before she could decide if she wanted to be honest, Thinker spoke to them. *"He's found our hunting party. Or rather, his proxies have."*

"You want us to go there," Transmuter asked, "now that we know she can teleport more than just herself?"

Traveler was about to say something about being volunteered for the task, then thought better of it. She found she was eager for it. She wanted another chance at them, and she could tell Transmuter was just as eager for a fight.

As if sensing their anticipation, Thinker said, *"Not yet. I think it's time to see what our mind-controlling friend is capable of. If how he pursued Traveler is any indication, he stands the best chance of taking care of the hunting party's most valuable asset."*

"Which is?" she asked.

"The woman in the tactical vest—the one running static

with my locating abilities who can make the others invisible. Once she's taken out, the others can be singled out much more easily."

"But she's not the leader, is she?" Transmuter said. "The red-headed man is. He almost killed Talker."

"He certainly is dangerous. His skills cannot be underestimated. But he can only neutralize one of us at a time, and only if he's in the same area physically. Without the rest of the group, he will be overwhelmed by us, which is a situation I don't think he's encountered before. Together, the hunting party is dangerous, but each is too dependent on the other. Separately, they cannot stand. If we take out the cloaker, there will be nowhere they can hide."

Traveler and Transmuter glanced at the figure twitching and muttering in the chair.

"Okay," she said, "let's see what he can do."

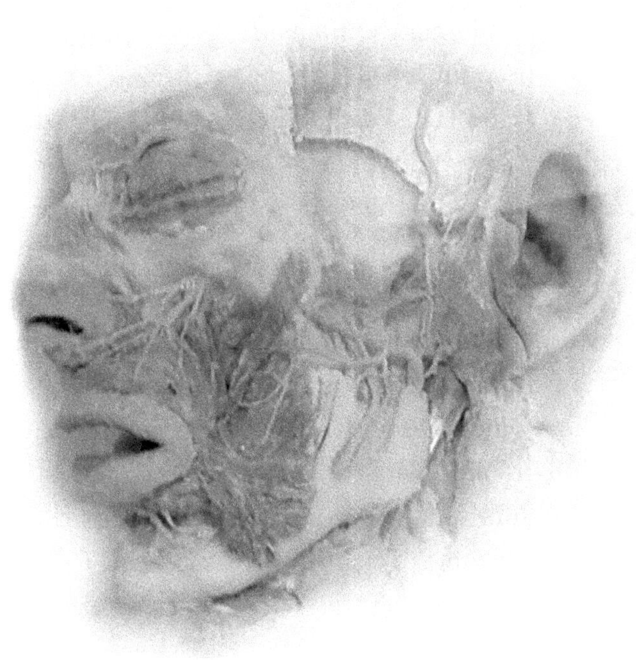

TWENTY

Talker did something he'd never done before; he called in every ounce of influence he had, pulled every string he could, all to bring down the full force of his army upon the hunting party. The time for cloak and dagger was over.

He was somewhat surprised when he realized he had never attempted this before. Perhaps, if he was honest with himself, he was afraid it would burn him out. Or that he just wasn't capable of such a feat, despite what he'd managed to do to track Traveler. But now he would bring down the fist of his power to pulverize those who had burned his home and nearly killed him. All the hunting party's little powers would only be so useful against human opponents. They could only kill so many before becoming overwhelmed. Ultimately, though, he just needed to kill Black Vest. The rest could be handled later. Even with her invisibility, they couldn't hide for long from hundreds of eyes, from the birds in the air and the rats in the walls.

But first, he needed to draw upon his human allies. The animals were nothing to command, but turning his influence over humans into a killing force was trickier. Though he had several who would follow his every command, no matter how atrocious, many more were simply eyes and ears who he had influenced so subtly that they weren't even aware the voice in the back of their minds wasn't just themselves. Talker would have to push them to his goal by any means necessary, even if that shattered them in the process.

One by one, he tumbled down the barriers, pulled and pushed, ripped and shouted and cajoled, until every human subject he had a significant toehold on received his instructions to hunt down the party and inflict as much damage as possible, especially against the one in the black vest, the one with graying hair. The effort strained the foundations of his mind, sending tremors through all his neat mental barriers, and somewhere he was dimly aware of his physical body shuddering and teeth chattering. But still he pushed, and his army rose.

In a small bungalow near the edge of town, Detective Simmons stood up from his recliner where he had been having a beer and watching late night TV. His wife had left, taking their son with her, and he couldn't sleep. Now, as if sleepwalking, he went to the bedroom, dressed carefully in his best charcoal suit, and loaded his service-issue Glock, stuffing extra magazines into the pockets of his jacket. Before he left, he grabbed the 12-gauge riot shotgun he kept under the bed. He headed out, red siren flashing on the dash of his battered Crown Victoria the whole way.

Across town, at the nearby military base, Sgt. Angie Carver got out of her bunk where she had been reading, quietly cut the throat of the quartermaster on duty, and filled two canvas bags with assault rifles and grenades. By the time she made it to her car, she had a nosebleed and was partially blind in her right eye. But she would last long enough.

A husband rose from beside his wife in bed and went out to the driveway to start his pickup. A short time later, he crashed it into the display window of a hunting and outdoor supply store. He broke his arm and rendered the truck inoperable, but others who were more able-bodied soon showed up, carrying away guns, knives, machetes, camping axes. Some of them were cops. One was a city councilwoman.

The birds in the sky fell to Talker's command. The rats scampered and the dogs howled and the bats beat their wings. He sent them all in a wave toward the basement window. It took them nearly half an hour to converge on the building, but he didn't wait until they all arrived to start the assault. He was afraid that if he hung back for too long, Broken Nose would sense his presence, and they would retaliate. Instead, he sent birds crashing against the windows of the building like kamikaze pilots, and he made his first few armed responders fall upon the main door. Some of the more pliant ones he could make hurt themselves with no regard for fatal injury crawled through the broken shards in the shattered window, cascading in like a living wave. The few still not armed with kitchen knives or the contents of a toolbox hurled themselves at the hunting party with ripping hands and tearing teeth.

The first wave was coordinated and overwhelming, and it needed to be, because the hunting party responded within seconds. Broken Nose was already standing up, looking spooked despite being armed with a submachine gun. She had obviously sensed some danger, but in the hunting party's weakened state, she didn't sense the sheer magnitude of that threat. Rifleman had been sitting at a table cleaning an array of weapons that wouldn't be out of place in a SWAT team armory, his head wrapped in bandages like a mummy. He sprang to his feet, a single-minded golem, his bulk pushing the armament-laden table forward. Black Vest had been oiling what looked like a falchion, a grim frown on her heat-chapped face. Professor, of course, had been lounging on a run-down sofa with an obscure-looking occult tome, one of his hands in a medical brace. He tossed the volume down without regard and used his good hand to draw his heavy chrome pistol from its holster.

Through the eyes of his proxies, he saw something delicious spring into their eyes. It wasn't fear—after all, they had seen and fought far more than the average human could ever imagine—but something close to panic, which was exactly what he wanted.

After that first wave, Talker's vision became jumbled, the scene viewed like the images in a rapidly whirling slideshow, as he switched perspective not only to monitor the area, but also as his proxies were cut down. The hunting party brought themselves up to speed quickly; he had to give them that. Even injured and caught in a moment of relative repose, they struck like a disturbed nest of hornets. A mangy gray dog managed to barely close its teeth around Black Vest's calf before she swung down her falchion, severing the animal's head. Broken Nose opened fire with the Swedish K submachine gun she had been holding, jamming its wire stock against her shoulder and raking the burst back and forth over the shattered window and its intruders until the magazine ran empty.

Outside, one of Talker's proxies had scaled the fire escape of a nearby building and set up with a scoped hunting rifle. Through the scope, Talker saw thick smoke billowing out of the basement window. He dimly hoped a fire had started, but switching to the view of an unnoticed rat, he quickly discovered Professor had tossed down a smoke grenade to facilitate their escape. This momentarily frustrated Talker, but no matter: more of his proxies were arriving, and all possible exits were covered. But what if they had some sort of escape tunnel?

Thinking fast, he sent his legion of rats scattering into the surrounding sewers to stand guard. But those pathways remained clear.

A door opened on the east side of the building, and the quartet spilled out, still somewhat teary-eyed from the smoke, but armed and moving fast. Talker's proxies converged on that side of the building, and the ones armed with handheld weapons were sent in a mass rush, along with whatever animals were available.

Professor tossed another grenade toward the oncoming crowd, this one a flashbang. The ensuing burst of phosphorescence blinded several of his proxies, putting a gap in his vision. This distraction gave Rifleman a chance to open fire on them. He wielded a massive drum-fed shotgun, and the weapon bucked against his massive shoulder as the automatic fire rained buckshot on their pursuers. The proxies kicked up chunks of concrete and brick with their ineffective return fire, but even though the hunting party was better trained, they knew if they stood their ground they would be overwhelmed. Closing ranks, they huddled around Black Vest, pressed their free hands on her, and disappeared.

The cloaking effect wasn't quite as successful this time, probably due to the multitude of perspectives and the weakened and panicked state of the group. Instead of being invisible, they appeared as a waver, like a heat mirage. The spot of refracted air bounced around like a will-o'-the-wisp, moving away from the building, and despite Talker's many eyes, he stood the risk of losing them.

Then Sgt. Carver began throwing her concussion grenades.

She pulled the pins and hurled them as fast as she could. Despite her blinded eye and consequent loss of depth perception, she maintained a fair accuracy, though her efficacy was just as much due to her complete lack of regard as to whether the blast killed friend or foe. The third grenade destroyed enough windows that an alarm sounded in one of the warehouses, thus ensuring the eventual arrival of the police. His plants could interfere, but only for so long. All the gunfire would attract enough attention on its own, even in this non-residential area. Swarms of bats and crows battered the hunting party, even as they were struck out of the sky by an invisible hand, undoubtedly Black Vest's blades and the scattered pellets of Rifleman's shotgun.

Luckily, the fourth grenade found its mark, and the group crystallized into view. Black Vest had gone down on one knee, and the falchion had fallen from her grasp as she clutched at her neck, where a piece of shrapnel had opened it up. Blood gushed from between her fingers, but she unsheathed the cavalry saber at her waist and used it to leverage herself up. Professor grabbed her, and as the group ducked into a side alley, Talker knew this was his last chance to get his quarry. The sustained control was taxing his already drained resources, and he was burning through his assets, not only from them being felled by the hunting party, but from their bodies and minds being overloaded by his heavy-handed control.

A few of his proxies had grabbed assault rifles from Sgt. Carver's bag and were lurching toward the alley on unsteady feet. "Go, you bastards, go," Talker heard his own voice say way back at Thinker's house, then refocused his control, temporarily dismissing even this diminished acknowledgment of self.

Through the eyes of a bird perched near the mouth of the alley, Talker saw the hunting party had gained a significant head start on his advancing proxies, even with Black Vest's injury slowing them down. They exited the alley and made their way toward a car coming up the side street from the north. As it approached, Rifleman stepped out into the street, his bulk and the enormous shotgun he held quite an incentive to stop.

But Talker knew who was in the car, an old Crown Victoria, and smiled.

The car screeched to a halt in front of the group, and the others made their way to the passenger's side, intent on leaving Rifleman the task of dealing with the driver. No sooner had they stepped off the curb than the driver's door flew open, and Broken Nose's head snapped to attention. She sensed the danger a mere moment before the others, her ability dismissed by the fight and her injuries. She brought up her submachine gun, but Detective Simmons was already standing, the left side of his face slack with palsy but his hands holding the Mossberg shotgun steady. Without hesitation, he squeezed the trigger, hitting Black Vest in the exposed area of her stomach below the hem of her tactical vest. A split second later, a hail of bullets from the submachine gun tore into the detective's chest, sending him crumpling to the ground.

The remaining three members of the hunting party crowded around their fallen member despite the stray bullets whizzing above their heads. Professor examined her grievous wounds before looking up at the others and shaking his head. He placed his hand briefly on Black Vest's graying hair. "I'm sorry, old friend."

As Professor crowded into the detective's car, Rifleman turned toward the alley, roaring in fury, the sweat-soaked bandages on his head unraveling like bloodied streamers. He emptied the drum magazine into the alley, his tremendous strength controlling the weapon's climb. At the driver's side of the car, Broken Nose bent down to take the detective's shotgun and pistol, but just as she was about to stand and turn to get behind the wheel, she paused, then leaned closer. She noticed then what Talker already knew and was hoping she wouldn't see: Detective Simmons was still alive, seconds from drawing his last breath but still among the living.

Through the policeman's failing vision, Talker saw the woman's bloodied face break into a broad smile as she crouched next to the body. Talker sent all his commands into Detective Simmons, willing him to shut down his remaining brain function. The strength of his focus made the remaining proxies in the alley falter, but it was all for nothing. Broken Nose tugged off her leather glove and placed it against Simmons's forehead. Talker could *feel* her cold fingertips digging into the skin, burrowing, and he knew then that she had found him, had found the house. Then she reached out and used two fingers to slowly close the detective's eyes, and a black screen fell across Talker's vision. *All* his visions.

Back at the house, he jolted out of the chair, sending it hurtling out behind him. As soon as he stood, though, the exertion of his assault and his already weakened state brought him down to one knee. Traveler and Transmuter were immediately at his side, helping him to his feet.

"I got her," he said. "My proxies did their task. Black Vest is dead."

"He actually did it?" Transmuter asked, his question clearly directed to Thinker.

"He's right," Thinker said in their minds. *"I can see them all clearly. The static is lifted. There will be no escape for them now."*

"So why don't we finish them off?" Traveler asked. "They're weak and on the run. If Talker can do this much, then surely we can take care of the rest of them."

Thinker didn't answer, and didn't have to, because Talker himself provided the next bit of information. "They know where we are," he said. "And though I can't access my proxies right now, I'm sure the hunting party is on their way here."

Both Traveler and Transmuter glared at him, as if this fact was enough to negate that he had single-handedly dealt with one of their greatest threats. Thankfully, Thinker came to his defense.

"Worry not. This is all according to plan. I knew attacking them directly would give the hunting party an opportunity to find out where we are. That is precisely how I wanted it to be. Without their shielder, I can pinpoint them anywhere. And with them fighting us here, we will have the advantage. They know we will, but they don't care. They want to see us dead now more than ever."

"I still don't understand why we can't take the fight to them," Traveler said.

"Because it isn't time to expose ourselves," Transmuter answered. "We have to prepare before we show ourselves to the world. Talker's attack was just people. That can be explained away. Bizarre, but just people, and people always find a way to smooth those things over. But if we show up teleporting and shapeshifting in front of people, that will begin it. And we want to begin it on our terms, not in reaction to a threat."

"How eloquent we've gotten," Talker said, but inside he had to concede the point. He sat down at a nearby table and was going about the futile task of straightening his bloody, ruined shirt. They all looked like a wreck, actually: bloodied and torn, with only Transmuter looking natural like that.

"Can you see into the minds of the hunting party?" Talker asked. "Who exactly are these people?"

"I can see much more than previously," Thinker said. *"But it's jumbled and incoherent, even for me. I get general impressions, with the occasional details. They've been operating as a quartet for quite some time, traveling back and forth across the country. At one point there was another member in their group—an old man with a white beard, but our kind killed him, and they've just been the four ever since. I can't see into their past—they've thoroughly walled that off— but I see their motivations. They are ruthless and relentless. They once burned down an entire apartment building full of people to flush out one of our kind who was hiding in the walls. They don't want to kill us to protect innocents or make the world a safer place. They kill us because that is what they do, what they were made to do. It's their destiny. And it will be our job tonight to make sure they die for their cause."*

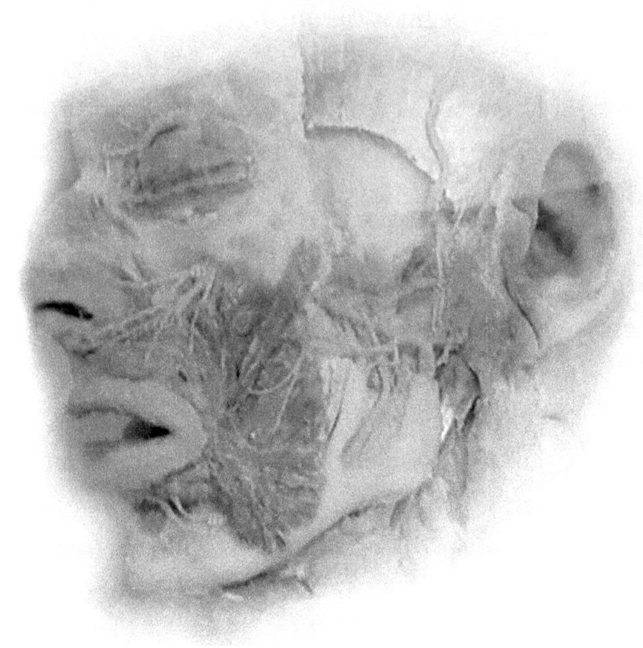

TWENTY-ONE

It took almost two hours before the hunting party approached the house. All the while, Thinker kept the others abreast of the group's activity, telling them the hunting party had fallen back to another safehouse in the city. It was a smaller, rudimentary locale, but there they applied first aid to their various wounds.

Professor had been grazed by a bullet across the shoulder, deep enough to require Rifleman to apply crude butterfly stitches. Broken Nose let the other members of the hunting party know, with clinical observation, that she was now partially deaf in her right ear from a nearby grenade detonation, and she had suffered numerous shrapnel wounds.

She had broken her left ring and pinky fingers to match her nose, both of which she hastily bound with splints. Rifleman bore the most injuries, having been hit with gunfire three times. But he didn't seem affected by it much, staunching and cauterizing the holes. Then he replaced the loose bandages on his blistered face with fresh gauze, covering his entire head with a blue ski mask adorned with an absurd teal pom-pom on the crown afterward.

They resupplied their weapons, upgrading to the heaviest firepower they could. Rifleman traded his now empty shotgun for a Milkor grenade launcher, and Broken Nose produced an antique-looking but well-maintained Thompson submachine gun, complete with a drum magazine and wooden foregrip. Professor strapped on a .50-caliber Desert Eagle and added several esoteric magical items to his carry bag.

But one thing they saw the hunting party *didn't* do: mourn. Despite Professor's parting words, none of them spoke of their departed member. Or even spoke at all. Transmuter seemed to be particularly unsettled by their grim silence, despite often preferring to keep his own counsel. The hunting party moved like automatons, and for a moment, Talker mused that this was exactly what they were: puppets being controlled by some larger intelligence, extensions of a greater will. And though it was an idle consideration, who knew? It made just as much sense as anything else they had encountered. Hunting parties were rare, but they weren't unique. The behavior of this group particularly chilled them, as despite their recent defeats, they remained especially formidable.

Though allowing the hunting party time to resupply and

lick their wounds seemed foolish, it was all part of the plan. After all, how could they prove the strength of their quartet unless they allowed their opponent a fair shot? Both groups had struck and wounded each other. The hunting party was now down a member, but they had experience working together as a team, even if a missing member of that team skewed some of their strategies.

Once the hunting party left to make their way to the house, the group gathered for one more conference. Traveler, Talker and Transmuter stood around the table at which they had first gathered. They might still have a bedraggled appearance, but they were not beaten down. They burned with a new purpose, because despite all their talking and their previous fights with the hunting party, this was the first time they would encounter them all together.

Talker was the only one of the group who looked truly worse for the wear. He still chose to sit, and his blanched complexion and shaky frame did not bode well for his performance.

"I don't need to be a mind reader to know what all of you are thinking," he said, acknowledging the twin looks of Traveler and Transmuter. "What I just did was the hardest I've pushed myself that I can remember, and it came at a considerable loss. I'm recovering without the benefit of blood to accelerate the process. But don't worry... I'll be ready once they get here. I'm not through with them yet."

Once that was addressed, Thinker spoke in their minds, and they noticed even Traveler now was comfortable with the mental communication, no longer prickling under the contact.

"We do not have much time," they said. *"So we must act quickly. What I'm about to ask each of you to do will not be easy. If we had more time, I would be content with letting the process play out more naturally. But we no longer have that option. I want the three of you to join hands—"*

Talker let out a dry bark of laughter, and Transmuter leveled a baleful glare at him, before grasping Talker's free right hand, enveloping it in a hand the size of a great ape's, with bristly hair and blackened nails.

"Join hands and open your minds. To me. To each other. Touch that alien core inside yourselves, the black hole that howls inside this human shell. It's there. It's what we really are."

Traveler reached out and took Talker's left hand, her grip decisive and no less fierce than Transmuter's even without the claws. With her left hand, she closed the link with Transmuter, her grip somewhat kindlier, if their kind were capable of that.

None of them closed their eyes. They didn't need much meditation to touch the dark heart Thinker had referred to. It was a hungry whirlpool, sucking in everything it could with the relentless pull of gravity. No matter how much it took— blood, fear, memories, loyalty—it would never be enough. That bottomless, yawning mouth would never be sated.

"Recognize that darkness," Thinker said. *"Recognize that in each of us, it is the same, because in each of us it contains the totality of all of us. That's what we need to tap into now, what we are capable of becoming."*

They resonated like plucked strings from a chord. The combined power of Talker and Thinker's mental abilities, of

Transmuter's protean nature, and Traveler's command of space, came together, flowed, and melted. For a moment, they all saw that grand design they were destined to fulfill. It came into view only briefly, like the flash of a photographer's bulb, then faded.

They came fully back into themselves. They looked around, slightly dazed, and Traveler said, "Was that..." Seemingly unsure of how to articulate what she had seen, Thinker knew.

"*Yes, it was,*" Thinker answered. "*That and more. Now, let's take our positions. Our guests will arrive shortly. We don't want to be poor hosts now, do we?*"

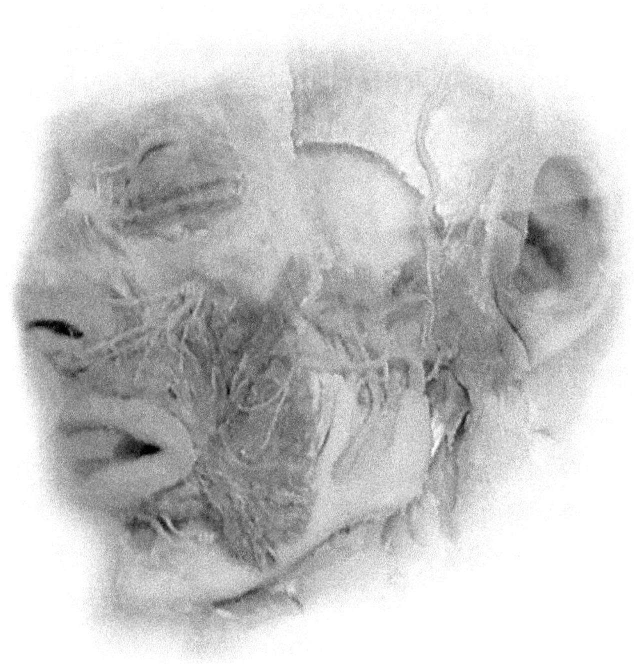

TWENTY-TWO

The house stood waiting in the night, except it wasn't quite night anymore. The first gray streaks of dawn began to lighten the horizon, and the twinkle of stars had faded to motes of dust in the slate blue sky. But the house was no longer the shabby crypt it had been mere weeks ago. It had not restored itself to the Gothic monstrosity Traveler had seen, but that had been a mere illusion anyway. This time, it was real. The facade of wood had taken on a fresh luster, filling in holes chewed by termites and burrowing rats. The shattered windows slowly filled their panes like small pools of water freezing over. Decades of dust blew away, as if propelled by a breath from a massive set of lungs.

The hunting party came on foot from the north side, cutting through the small copse there. Thinker saw them moving silently, and a peek into their minds confirmed that although they didn't know for sure they were being spied on, they assumed it. Especially Broken Nose. But more importantly, Thinker saw that they didn't care. There was something more going on to their motivation than revenge or bloodthirst, though its full meaning remained obscured. There were still some frustrating blind spots. But no matter. Soon whatever little thoughts they had rattling around in their skulls would be irrelevant.

Traveler could also see them from her vantage spot on the roof.

"Not yet?" she asked Thinker, her eyes locking on them through the trees, preparing herself to appear behind the hunting party at a moment's notice.

"Let them come," Thinker said. *"Like pilgrims. Like supplicants. The first witnesses."*

Talker and Transmuter waited inside. Talker was quietly gathering his strength while Transmuter paced, his body already rippling and contorting only to pull itself back into its neutral form. He shrugged out of his ruined denim jacket and tossed it over the back of the nearby couch. The muscles spasmed under his taut, filthy skin, patches of fur or scales bristling randomly, then retreating.

"Nervous?" Talker asked puckishly.

Transmuter stopped pacing long enough to look at him, though it fell short of being a glare. "I know you're planning on killing me if you have the chance," he said bluntly. "That's okay. You're welcome to try."

Thinker could sense, with their new clarity and connection to the group, that Talker was taken aback. It must have been such a very long time since anyone had threatened him, in ignorance or otherwise. "Why do you—" he began, then caught himself. What had he been about to say, Thinker speculated? *Why do you not like me? Why do you feel the need to try and humiliate me? You show deference for Thinker, and respect for Traveler. Why do you single me out?*

For a shining moment, Talker's mind in all its labyrinthine machinations was opened to Thinker, and they could clearly see his feelings and thoughts. The emotion of genuine respect was something utterly alien to him. He knew the definition of the word intellectually, same as words like *love* or *happiness*. But as an actual emotion, he couldn't imagine it. He had commanded others to listen and obey, had ripped fealty from their lips, but not once had anyone expressed a genuine emotion toward him that wasn't fear or thinly veiled hatred. Even others like him had treated him with caution and suspicion. The trio was the first he'd been around that interacted with him however they wished.

"What?" Transmuter asked, daring him to finish his unspoken thought.

But the conversation was cut short. The front door exploded, sending a wave of heat and splinters into the foyer. Rifleman had fired the first shot from the Milkor grenade launcher. The blast sent Talker sprawling, but Transmuter was ready, dissipating and letting his own biocloud mingle with the dust and debris. Thinker saw Talker's thought flitter by briefly wondering if the grenade hurt Thinker, since their consciousness and the house were fused like mind and body.

"It does," they said in his mind. *"But I'll survive. I always do."*

"And the rest of us?" he asked, standing up and brushing the splinters off. "The other two are your warriors, but what part do I play in this? My proxies are spent. I don't even know if I have the strength right now to infiltrate their minds, and even if I did, that big fucker with the grenade launcher is the only one I could actually get to. So what, am I…bait?"

"Trust me," they said, aware of the request's inherent irony. *"Believe me. There's a place for you in our future plans. And the current one. Come down to the basement. We have a few final things to prepare."*

Outside came the burst of a submachine gun, a heavy chugging sound pounding through the night. Not needing further incentive, Talker made for the now repaired basement steps.

The hunting party, meanwhile, had moved in closer after Rifleman had expended his exploratory shot. Traveler had flicked in and out of space several yards away from them, clearly a feint, though Broken Nose had chanced a volley in her direction.

"Goddamn teleporter," Broken Nose said. "She could pop in front of us at any time. Why isn't she attacking?"

"Toying with us," Professor said. "Trying to get a feel for how to engage."

"Next shot I got in the drum is phosphorus," Rifleman said, already putting the grenade launcher to his shoulder. "You want me to shoot another at the house?"

"No, wait. Not yet," Professor said. "I'm trying to get a read on this house. There's something not right about it, something hard to pin down. If we can just get a little closer, I might be able to neutralize it."

A rush of air wafted over them, carrying with it the scent of blood and leather, the crackle of animal insanity. None of them had to turn to see that the pale woman had appeared before them, but still Professor tried, whirling his pistol toward her and beginning the mutter of an incantation under his breath. But it was as if the air was filled with tar; his arm seemed to physically stick to the darkness of the night. She was so fast, so unholy fast, and before Professor could finish his curse or pull the trigger, before he could neutralize her power, she had seized the arm of his coat and pulled him into the void.

Rifleman roared and turned frantically in circles, screaming, "Where did she take him? *Where the fuck did she take him?*"

Broken Nose tried to catch his attention, trying to tell him that Professor was alive somewhere in the house because she could still sense his presence. But for all his prowess, a berserker panic overtook the hulking man. He put the grenade launcher to his shoulder and sent three shots rapidly into the facade of the house—two phosphorus and one nasty explosive called a Hellhound—lighting it up with a searing white flame that consumed the front door and windows. Broken Nose thought she heard an echo in her head for a moment, like an animal growling in pain. This time she managed to get his attention.

"It's the house itself," she said. "It's sentient. It can feel pain. If we can destroy the house, then we can take them out."

"But what about—"Rifleman began, but she cut him off.

"I know, and that means we've got to get inside and get him out. You find and extract him while I plant the charges."

Rifleman nodded, his rage placated for the moment, and the two rapidly closed the distance between them and the house. But though they noticed the flames were rapidly diminishing, as if the house were absorbing them, they did not notice the oily fog gathering around their ankles. Not until the mist began to solidify into ropy strands, like a spider's web, and seized Rifleman around the legs, yanking him off balance but not quite bringing him off his feet.

Broken Nose leveled the Thompson at the solidifying mass and squeezed off a long burst, raking it back and forth across the vaguely humanoid shape, kicking up a burst of cold dirt and rock as the heavy bullets passed through it without much effect. Growling, she reached into the pocket of her coat for some other weapon, but Rifleman stopped her.

"Get to the house!" he barked, struggling with the encroaching mass like a man fighting a giant python. "Plant the charges!"

Without a moment's hesitation or concern for her compatriot, she bounded across the lawn toward the house, which was still smoldering but no longer ignited.

Transmuter didn't give chase. It was part of the plan to get them into the house, just scattered. He was even keeping his current transformation slow, allowing the Rifleman enough edge that he thought he was accomplishing something. Once he got the mental acknowledgment from Traveler that Broken Nose was inside the house, he pulled back from his captive and resumed his baseline form.

The large man sprang quickly to his feet, regaining his balance with a preternatural agility. His hand dove to a large pouch at his side, presumably to draw his secondary firearm.

"Oh, come on," Transmuter chided with amusement. "Do you really think that's going to do anything against me?"

Instead of a pistol, Rifleman drew a small spray canister, similar to a tear gas fogger. He depressed the trigger while whipping his arm back and forth, sending a mist of stinging liquid toward Transmuter. Reflexes dulled by confidence, Transmuter wasn't fast enough to dodge, and he couldn't absorb or phase through it like a bullet. The particles settled on his skin, smoking as it found purchase and ate away at him, releasing a septic smell like old infections and desecrated graveyards. The bastard had just sprayed him with acid. The substance momentarily blinded him, and he howled in shock and frustration. He went incorporeal, which didn't relieve him but instead made even more of his cells mix with the acidic fog.

He drifted into the earth, spreading himself among the wet dirt. The acid had momentarily clouded his link with Thinker, but now he once again found that steady, always rational voice.

"Hold fast. He hasn't gotten the better of you yet, has he?"

Transmuter shifted his form, hiding an emotion close to something he hadn't felt in a very long time—embarrassment? Shame?—and charged toward the house, already healing, pushing away earth with mole-like claws. He knew he could have stayed in his non-solid form and moved through the ground much more quickly, but he wanted to stay in a body. Somehow his substance let him hang on to the anger. He wasn't done with Rifleman yet.

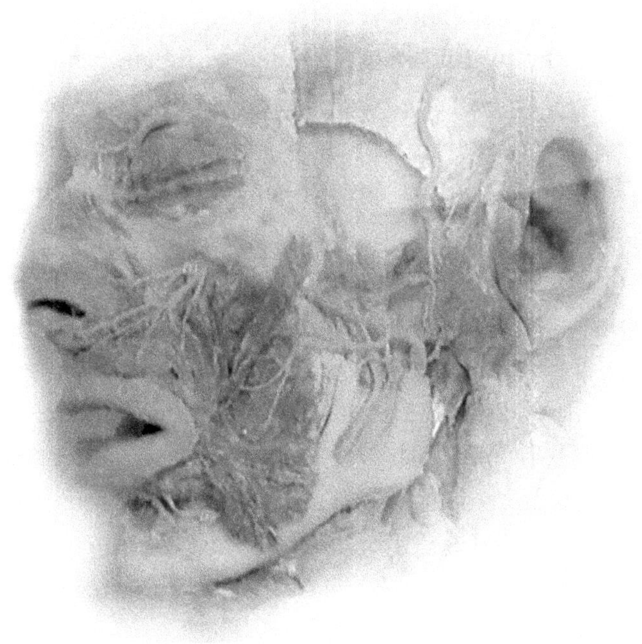

TWENTY-THREE

After spurring Transmuter into continuing his pursuit of Rifleman, Thinker turned their attention—or at least the priority of their attention—back to the basement, what they thought of as their neural core. Just moments earlier, Traveler had appeared, carrying Professor with her. The man looked equally bewildered and enraged, his face a mask of purple rage that barely hid the disorientation and fear at being carried through Traveler's howling void, even for a split second.

After dumping him on the floor, she nodded in acknowledgment and disappeared just as quickly as she had appeared, off to handle Broken Nose, who was just now reaching the house. She even spared a glance to Talker, who stood near the pit and had managed to regain a modicum of his dignity. None of them needed to exchange a word. They barely even needed to articulate thoughts. Their collective mind was beginning to truly form, an entity *of* them and *beyond* them.

Professor stood up ramrod straight, the rage diminishing from his face, taking on a more calculating look. Thinker could only scan the surface of his thoughts, which meant he hadn't fully committed to neutralizing Thinker's mental threat. Surely he was at the very least blunting Talker's abilities as well, already evident from Talker's contemptuous sneer. But Professor's divided attention couldn't last for much longer. He hadn't had time to neutralize Traveler, and to do so mid-jump would have been tantamount to suicide.

"You bastards," he said, pointing the heavy Desert Eagle at Talker, who, unlike Thinker, at least had a physical form to threaten. He sounded more exasperated than outraged. Thinker could feel Talker pushing for control, eager to rip the man's mind apart like a black-eyed seagull working at an oyster. Thinker felt Professor's spike of fear at realizing Talker's overwhelming, sadistic malice, and the red-headed man made the decision to fully commit to suppressing Talker's abilities—and that was his mistake.

Professor's mind opened to Thinker like a blossoming flower of infinite complexity, like an intricate clock with each gear and spring lovingly laid out on white cloth. There was drive, and a singularity of purpose, and fierce intelligence. But there were also things that weren't there, things even the most basic and degraded human had—simple animal needs and emotions whose absence loomed like unimaginable chasms. And for the first time since the beginning of the endeavor, Thinker was taken aback.

"What happened to you?" they asked in Professor's mind. The man only grinned in response, as if he had delivered a carefully constructed punchline.

Talker stepped forward, sensing something was wrong, but before he could speak, a long, fierce clatter of submachine gun fire came from upstairs.

Broken Nose had been working fast, planting charges of C-4 in key places on the ground floor, knowing that she had a mere handful of minutes, perhaps even seconds. She couldn't be sure who was dead yet, with this wretched place somehow dampening the lifeforms she normally felt. A choking psychic smog obscured her senses, and with another member of the team gone, she had no way to counter it. She had to redouble her efforts to stay clear and sane. The consciousness in the house pushed against her reality, complicating the passageways into twisted, maze-like turns, swelling the walls like distended bellies as blood leaked from cracks in the plaster.

"C'mon," she said, arming the fifth charge. "I know that's bullshit. Do you think I care if you turn me around in circles? That I've planted explosives in the same spot? You think I even care if I blow myself up?"

"I think you do," a voice said, echoing down the long passageway.

Broken Nose stood up, raising her Thompson and sending a stream of bullets without thought. The gun kicked against her shoulder and climbed toward the ceiling. Once the spots in her eyes started to clear, she saw the scarecrow figure of the teleporter. The messy fringes of her hair stuck out like the quills of a porcupine, and her leather jacket billowed in the still air. She floated a foot off the floor, drifting toward her with the languid presence of a jellyfish.

"I didn't need to disappear to avoid the bullets," the teleporter said. "I can just push them out of the way now, no matter how fast you spit them at me. I could probably completely stop them. I'm much stronger now. See?"

With that, the submachine gun was wrenched from Broken Nose's hands, nearly breaking her finger on the trigger guard. The weapon hung suspended in the air, then exploded. No, not exploded as she had first thought, but instantly dismantled, as if it had been broken down for cleaning, or for complete rebuilding. Fragments of wood and metal circled the air, and a line of fat .45-caliber bullets orbited the gun like an asteroid belt. The teleporter waved her hand dismissively, and the parts clattered to the floor, their fall curiously muted. Broken Nose looked down and saw the floor had become tacky, sucking at her feet, leaving strings of goo when she lifted her shoes.

Undeterred, she lifted the detonator to the explosives. Six would have to be enough. She had been honest earlier about not being afraid to obliterate herself. The force of the explosives would be enough to level the entire house and everything in it. It was a sacrifice she knew the remaining members of her group would be willing to make. This hive, this enclave, this forming corpus, was much too dangerous to be allowed a chance at survival.

The woman down the hallway seemed to realize what she was doing, and Broken Nose knew she couldn't hesitate, couldn't let the woman teleport away to a safe distance. She would be significantly less dangerous on her own, but her potential had been awakened, and she would go on to form another group as soon as she could.

In the microsecond it took to depress the trigger for the detonator, the world turned black. Cold hands seized her shoulders, materializing slowly like a developing photograph. Mesmerized by the apparition with pale statue hands and long, dirty nails and scarred knuckles, with a massive effort of will, Broken Nose took in her surroundings.

There was nothing there. Not just the obscuring cover of darkness, but a deep, absolute void. The figure of the teleporting woman floated in front of her, time moving sluggishly in whatever hellish place this was, even as she fought to finish pressing the trigger on the detonator in her hands. The teleporting woman snarled through sharp yellow teeth, her eyes glowing with sickly green fire. The detonator clicked home, but she didn't need the terrible woman's smirk to let her know she had failed.

The now useless detonator tumbled from her hands, drifting with the lazy descent of a snowflake. She glanced downward and saw the cavernous place of infinite darkness was not a void. Something was down there in the dark, as massive as a mountain, undulating and writhing. And she could see it, because the massive thing glowed with its own faint light. She knew she would go mad if she touched it, if she even looked at it any longer than she had to. But the teleporter had already let go of her arm, and she was falling, her screams swallowed in the vacuum.

Traveler reappeared in the hallway and immediately slumped against the wall. Why had she done that? She could have teleported the woman to the bottom of a lake, and she would have still been effectively out of range. Why, especially now, did she feel the impulse to do something so risky?

Because now I'm not scared of anything, she thought. She teleported down to the basement. Transmuter should be finished soon.

Rifleman recovered his grenade launcher and made his way toward the house in massive, indefatigable strides. He resisted the urge to empty the rest of the cylinder into the house, not wanting to risk incapacitating his remaining compatriots. Besides, he knew despite his trick with the acid, the shapeshifter wouldn't be far behind. And he might need the weapon to hold him off long enough to regroup with the others, if they were still alive.

The shapeshifter couldn't be stopped until the prime leader

had been destroyed, the one who had implanted the gestalt idea in their heads. The corrupting influence of the idea had to be cut out like a tumor, and after that, the remaining members of the group would fall away, able to be picked off like the stupid, if dangerous, creatures they were. This group had come much further in a shorter time, but there was still time to stop it, methods to achieve that end be damned.

When Rifleman entered the still smoldering remains of the front door, he encountered a much different landscape than the subtle labyrinth used to obstruct Broken Nose. Rifleman had a much more direct methodology, so Thinker responded in kind, greeting the man with the exact depraved chamber of horrors he expected.

The parlor had been replaced with a torture theater. There was a rack decorated with an emaciated figure stretched until his limbs hung by mere skin and ligament, an Iron Maiden floating in a pool of blood with a feeble scream rattling in its bowels, and corpses in various states of decay packed in gibbets dangling from the vaulted ceiling. Decorated with flayed skins like heavy tapestries, the walls were made of stacked up skulls used as bricks. Thinker found it all very crass, but the smut book Inquisition scene was doing its job. The mountain of a man, that relentless hunting dog, actually gasped and took a step back, unprepared for the scene after what he had witnessed at Talker's bungalow.

Transmuter's hands burst through the threshold bottom,

not phasing but tearing through it, his massive, many-fingered limbs seizing Rifleman by the ankles and sending him sprawling onto the bone-littered floor. The illusory bones crumbled to powder under his weight, the dust getting into his mouth but the balaclava prevented any inhalation. Despite the fall, he held on to the Milkor, but instead of firing it at Transmuter, who surged out of the hole in a geyser of spidery limbs and snapping jaws, Rifleman shot the phosphorus round at the ceiling of the room.

Thinker flinched, having to divert precious resources from dealing with Professor. The round had exploded in a flash of brilliance and now burned through the flesh of the house, searing its senses with white, radiant heat. Rifleman had been smart enough to close his eyes and look away, but Thinker doubted he had gotten away unscathed. The impairment caused by the bright light didn't stop him from quickly lobbing the next round—a Hellhound explosive—in Transmuter's direction.

The force of the blast was tremendous, disintegrating much of what remained of the house's front façade and scattering Transmuter across the lawn.

In the basement, Talker and Traveler looked up at the rapid one-two explosion and exchanged—for the first time— a mutual feeling of worry. But just as the vibrations from the explosion began to settle, the silence from Transmuter was broken by a screaming psychic roar of a wounded animal. It was then they knew the remaining member of the hunting party would be handled in short order.

Transmuter stepped through the ruined door, setting aside tricks for the moment and reverting to his baseline form. Among the settling dust, he saw Rifleman, astonishingly, getting to his feet. Fragments from the explosion had found him, turning his chest and arms into a jumble of cuts, blood, and singed clothing. Shards of metal and wood stuck out of his massive body, giving him a quilled appearance. The top of the balaclava smoldered, and the side of the mask, along with the left corner of his mouth, had split open into a gory gash, giving him the appearance of a rotten jack-o'-lantern. He had lost the grenade launcher when the explosion had knocked him back into the room, but as he regained his balance, Rifleman drew a thin-bladed trench knife from his belt, threading his fingers through its spiked brass knuckle handle.

Will he ever stop? Transmuter thought with a mix of alarm and admiration.

Rifleman leaped, an attacking panther, surging toward Transmuter with a madman's ferocity, and when he brought down the knife toward his skull, it was with the power of a jackhammer. But instead of connecting with skin and bone, the knife whistled through empty air. Transmuter's image had cleared away like a wisp of smoke. Even as Rifleman took time to process the difference, he whirled around, brandishing the trench knife, ready to confront whatever trap he had stumbled into.

The real Transmuter was already waiting for him. He had projected the illusion in front of Rifleman without even realizing what he was doing, and though it had only fooled him for a moment, that gave Transmuter the edge he finally needed. He phased his hand through Rifleman's chest and found his heart—strong and pumping with vitality, but still all too human—before solidifying again. He transformed the fist that held the man's heart into a tangle of barbs and watched the life finally, grudgingly, fade from his eyes, even as Rifleman made one last feeble swipe with the blade that nicked open Transmuter's chin.

Transmuter yanked his hand out of Rifleman's chest, letting the man's massive body crash among the ruins of the parlor. He stared at his bloodied hand before a multitude of small mouths appeared, lizard tongues flicking out to lap up the tacky mess.

"I've already taken care of the other one," he heard Traveler speak in his head. *"Get down to the basement. We have to finish this."*

"Did you see that?" he said, his voice almost choked with astonishment. "Did you see me project the illusion? I did it. Me." He suddenly threw up his hands like the jubilant attendee of a tent revival. *"I did it!"*

"And there will be more of that," Thinker said, and Transmuter thought he could detect a hint of pride in their voice. After all, he had been the first to throw in with the plan, however cautiously. Didn't it make sense that he would be the first to receive the promise fulfilled?

Thinker continued. *"We are becoming what we were always intended to be. But we have one last thing to do. Not an obstacle to clear, but an opportunity to seize."*

Transmuter surveyed the room. The explosive rounds had wrought considerable damage to the house, but even now the flickering flames were being smothered, and the burned and blasted pieces of the house—of Thinker—began to repair, just like their bodies could regenerate from grievous wounds. He saw wood regrowing, resolidifying itself like he could reassemble his cells. The shattered glass in the windows spun back together in a lattice as delicate as spiderwebs.

He spared a glance at the dead Rifleman with the gaping chest wound, the felled Goliath, and allowed himself another flush of satisfaction. Then he went incorporeal and drifted through the floor to emerge in the basement.

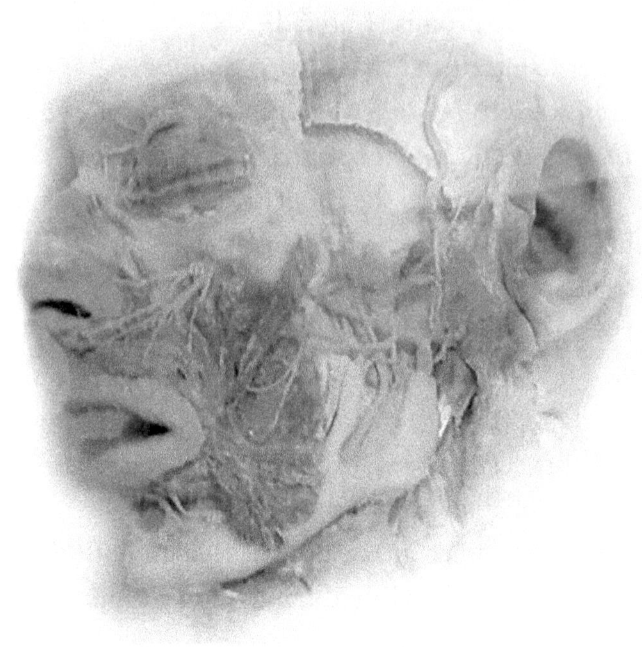

TWENTY-FOUR

Talker, in a moment of hospitality, had scrounged up a chair from the upstairs dining room, and he had shoved Professor into it. The man sank into himself, the wood straining under the weight of his defeat, his massive head of copper curls hanging down. His bowed head made him look like a dog waiting to be kicked. At his back was the house's heart—the pit Thinker had been prematurely interred in.

Once a ragged gash of pickaxed concrete, the opening had been reconstructed into a smooth, round hole, its edges done up in delicate tiles of shimmering opalescence to contrast with the sickly yellow-green light that sometimes pulsed from the hole itself. Thinker imagined that it did the Professor just as well that he didn't have to gaze into that maddening light on top of feeling its progenitor infiltrate his mind. With that added indignity, his impressive resilience in the face of unavoidable defeat might have completely collapsed. They needed him weakened, receptive, but not in pieces.

Talker, Traveler, and Transmuter stood in front of Professor, sizing him up like butchers one moment and then in the next staring at him with the open, curious gazes of a trio of schoolchildren.

Talker, still bearing the marks on his clothes of where Professor had tried to destroy him, glared at him with the kind of glee that can only come when revenge is consummated. Thinker considered it a good thing that Talker's obvious hate kept Professor's neutralization power focused on him. It would make things much easier.

Transmuter had pulled himself back together admirably after his confrontation with Rifleman, and he stood with bloodied bare chest and soot-crusted jeans, his muscles coiled like a jaguar waiting to pounce. And finally there was Traveler, always with her bemused grin, twisting the buckle of her coat's belt.

Thinker spoke in Professor's mind, but let the others hear as well.

"I want you to tell us everything you know. I already know it and could convey it to the others through our network, but I want them to hear it straight from you. It's quite pointless at this juncture to be uncooperative. I know you are a man of logic. Is that not so?"

"Yes," Professor said, his dignity not allowing him to

betray the resignation they all knew was there.

"How long has your group been pursuing us? How did you respond to us so quickly when we ourselves have only just recently become fully aware of each other?"

"The call you put out," he responded. Even in his defeat, Professor's creeping condescension made his given moniker more accurate than ever. "The others weren't the only ones to sense it. My associate, the one who could reverse the mind control—" He paused, his face twisting up. "Her name... I can't remember her real name. We worked together for almost three years, and I can't—"

"You've forgotten it," Thinker said bluntly. *"It was cleared out. You didn't even realize it was gone until you tried to recall it directly. We will get to that in a moment. Continue."*

Professor produced a handkerchief from his blazer pocket and wiped the sweat from his brow and mouth before continuing. "She could sense the call—in her dreams. And she had visions, hints of what was to come. That's why we were able to know you would gather here. She sensed the unspoken intent, knew you didn't just want help. Didn't just want to continue to exist. You wanted to build something more."

"Our...superorganism?" Thinker asked.

"Yes. And we knew how dangerous you all would be if you weren't stopped. That's why we had to become dangerous too. We didn't choose it. It was like—a mutation, a rapidly developed evolutionary response to circumstances. Just like none of you are consciously adopting each other's abilities."

"Then it really is happening to all of us?" Traveler asked.

Professor nodded solemnly. "It doesn't really do me much

good to try to suppress one of you in particular anymore, to be honest, since to some degree all of you now can do everything the others can do." He looked down at his feet and sighed. "We failed. We were supposed to stop you, and we failed. God knows what damage you'll inflict upon the world before someone else stops you."

"Tries to stop us," Transmuter said. "And we aren't doing damage. We're fulfilling our destinies."

Professor chuckled bitterly. "That's what makes you dangerous. It's one thing when you all were merely mindless creatures, hunting and feeding—just vermin. Only motorized instinct, even if that instinct is not of the natural world. But give you a creed? A philosophy? No, that must be stopped, whatever the risk. Whatever the cost."

"And you see now that you, none of you, can hope to stand against us?" Thinker asked. *"We have become more than beasts of simple hunger and cruelty. We now stand to finally benefit humanity. They need us."*

The defeated man brought up his heavy, leonine head once more, in one final act of defiance. Even his pragmatic and fatalistic mind could not deny the need at this moment.

"There used to be no 'us' and 'you.' Do you even realize that? Do you even remember things being different? Did you ever stop to ask yourselves, with all your grand plans and ambitions, not just why you're here, but *how* you're here? You didn't just spring into being from out of nowhere. Do you ever wonder why you can't remember?"

An invisible hand seized Professor's throat, and a multitude of small grasping things like the cold hands of dead children yanked at his hair.

"What are you talking about?" Traveler shouted, taking a step forward so big and clumsy that she almost lost her balance and toppled into him.

He managed to give a twisted smile. "You can *almost* remember on your own, can't you? You're relatively new to this, at least compared to the rest of your companions."

Transmuter spoke next. "He's saying we used to be human."

"Of course we were," Talker said impatiently, rapidly gaining back the imperious tone that had deserted him now that his enemies had been brought to heel. "I don't know what he's prattling on about us forgetting. I remember precisely who I used to be."

Professor laughed out loud at that, a booming roar that hinted to the passionate man he had perhaps once been. "You idiot," he said. "You don't know a damned thing. You tinker with people's minds. You possess them and rob them of their will. You've spent so long looking through the eyes of others that you've hijacked some of their memories. You built a patchwork quilt out of them and called them your own. Whatever memories you *think* are yours, that's not you."

Talker's stridency dropped away to a twisted snarl of rage, and he advanced on the man, prepared to commit violence himself for once. He grabbed Professor by his lapels and shook him, rattling the man's whole body and showing that despite his seemingly frail body and recent injuries, Talker still possessed strength greater than almost any human. "What the hell do you know?" he sneered. "What makes you so fucking smart?"

Regaining his poise, Professor spoke. "Because I know who you all are. Who all of you used to be."

Talker dropped him as if the man had become poisonous to the touch. Traveler merely wore the look of a horrible suspicion she didn't want confirmed.

"Is it true?" Transmuter asked Thinker. "You would know if he really knew anything or was just trying to bullshit us."

Thinker answered without hesitation. *"Yes, he does know. He's not lying."*

"So that means you know now, too," Traveler stated. "You read his mind, so now you know. So soon we will know, too. Know who we really are…were."

"Not necessarily," Thinker said. *"I'm holding on to the information. It's not easy holding it back, and I'm only able to do so because our group is still young."*

Traveler glanced at Professor with his manic, fatalistic smile and knew that this exchange did not include him.

"I want to give you all a choice," they said. *"You can know, satisfy your own curiosity, finally have that dead spot cleared up. Or…"*

Transmuter finished the thought. "Or…we can let go."

Moments passed as the group silently deliberated, causing Professor's smile to falter. What he had intended as his ace in the hole was not giving him the advantage for which he had hoped. Transmuter was the first to decide. He stepped forward and spoke directly to Professor. "It doesn't matter who or what I used to be. I don't care."

Traveler was close behind, nodding slowly, her eyes at first glazed and distant, but then hardening with resolve. "All that's gone. We're something else now. No undoing it. So who gives a damn."

Talker was the last to remain silent. Before the events of this night, he had been the one with the most power to lose, at least temporarily. But now he had been brought low, with nothing left to lose like the rest of them—nothing, at least, except the integrity of his purpose. They, at least, had no memories, and so had given up nothing except a vague hope. The integrity of Talker's mind and identity had been lost, so recently, and it would be very tempting for him to grasp at anything that might give that back. Giving that up, completely and irrevocably, would demonstrate a selflessness of purpose that frankly he seemed incapable of. When he spoke, though, it was not to the man huddled on the floor, but to Thinker.

"We might have a choice about whether we want to know or not, but you don't. You read his mind, so you know what you used to be. *Who* you used to be. So, what, can you just get rid of that? And if not, that gives you an advantage over us."

"What advantage could I possibly use that information for?" Thinker responded. *"Whatever little facts this man has collected, what slips of paper or notarized certificates he might have scrounged up, that's not who I am. I have created who I am, and the only me that matters is the one now. Whoever that was, how is that real? How is that me any more real than this me?"*

Talker nodded gravely, like someone who had received harsh but needed advice. He then wordlessly crossed the distance to Professor and seized him by the chin, pinching him with his long fingers, the yellow tapered nails digging into the flesh beneath the red beard.

"You tried to kill me," he said, his voice free now of animosity. "And I only think it's fair, since your group tried to lessen our numbers, that we add to our ranks instead." He looked up to the rest of the group. "What do you say? Are we in agreement?"

Professor trembled as Transmuter and Traveler approached. Whatever cavalier attitude he had managed to infuse in himself earlier vanished. They each laid one of their hands on Professor's shoulders: Traveler's bony, black-veined hand on his left, and Transmuter's boar-bristled claw on his right. They could feel the tweed fabric move up and down and Professor's body hitched with strangled sobs. Moments later, an unseen presence indented the thick red hair on the top of his head, in a depression that may have been that of a hand.

Talker asked, "How do we do this?"

A strange sound like a stalling engine sounded in their heads before they realized that Thinker was laughing. *"I can't claim to be all-knowing on this one. To my knowledge, I have never done this, nor can I directly remember anyone else who has. I only have supposition and instinct."*

Professor shook, eyes rolled up and bubbly yellow foam crusted the edge of his mouth. Whether they even meant it, the process had already begun.

"We must give a piece of ourselves, a piece of our…souls, for lack of a better word. Normally, it would be just one, but

this one will be different, born not of one, but of all. The first descendant of the Corpus."

Now that the idea had been implanted, it came to them as naturally as their original preternatural gifts, as easy as rearranging the cells or commanding the mind. An eldritch light formed around their heads, seeping from their orifices like ectoplasm, clouding around their heads in a nimbus. The light in the basement hole flared with a bizarre color and stank of old, dangerous magic and hungry madness. The house beneath their feet vibrated intensely as the light snaked down their arms, coiling and thickening, inching toward Professor, now entirely held upright by their hands.

The thick, sickly light gathered around his head, swirling and encasing it in a reverse birth caul, glowing until his features were obliterated into a semi-formless lump, like the rough figure a child would make out of clay. They felt something give way inside of themselves, physically felt a tear like a muscle, emotionally like—what? Loss? Heartbreak? Did they even remember what those words meant beyond the meager definitions? Finally, they let Professor fall limply upon the basement floor. The light had fully coalesced into a sac, writhing and tightening. He was not breathing.

They made their way upstairs, all of them silent, even Thinker. They hung their heads, weary and literally drained, torn and bloodied. Scents of burned wood and scorched flesh hung in the air. The smell wasn't reminiscent of injury and defeat, but of an offering made to blood-stained idols. The large gap in the front of the house let in something more than the crisp autumn air and greedy insects hovering over Rifleman's corpse. After decades of avoidance, the animals had returned. After all, the house had other things on its mind now.

In the sky, the clouds were a wash of red and pink, overall a shade lighter than the dark ultramarine or midnight blue they were used to. Stepping out onto the portico, Transmuter held up his hands and watched a golden beam dance across it that had broken through the branches of the trees. He waited dispassionately for his skin to start bubbling like it had when caught in Rifleman's acid spray, but his hand remained intact.

Traveler had joined him at his right. She reached up with both hands, as if she could catch the light in a way someone might gently enclose a butterfly, before putting her hands in the worn pockets of her jacket.

"Is this…" she began, then stared at the rising orb of fire in the sky.

Talker came up on Transmuter's left. Even he smiled, not a trace of a grimace.

The three stood at the threshold of their fourth, while their newest addition stayed in the depths, not dead but merely dreaming. They stood, braced against one another, their squabbles and paranoia forgotten, perhaps permanently, and watched the dawn rise upon what would be the first of many, many days.

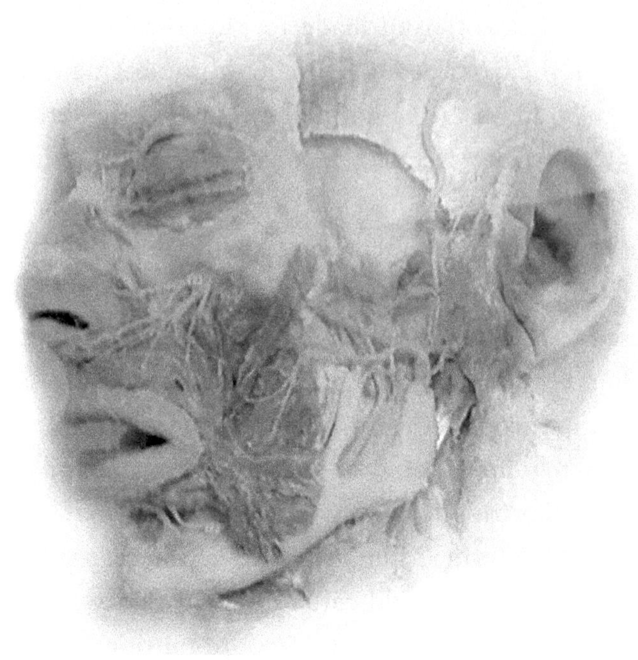

EPILOGUE

Time passed, but not much. Now that they had come together, things moved rapidly. The one who had once been Professor woke up, weak and confused. But he had others to help him through his transition, to build him up from the beginning to inherit his destiny. In a short amount of time, once he gathered his strength, they would see if he had retained his talent for neutralizing powers. Such an ability would be useful to add to their collective repertoire, especially if they came across others like him.

Talker grew gaunt and seemed on the verge of ossifying, but there was incredible strength in his frailty, and he worked tirelessly, sending out his emissaries, human and animal alike. They not only contained his will, but all their wills, and they spread out in a dragnet, looking for others like them, placing them on a mental map they all stored in their heads.

They didn't just rely on Talker's proxies. At the same time, a man walked the roads of the surrounding areas. He walked slowly, for he knew they had more time, enough time. He wore a clean suit in undertaker black, and he sported a neatly trimmed beard. His feet were bare, but clean, and only someone who got close enough would see that his feet in fact never touched the earth. He walked on, a missionary spreading the word, germinating the idea, taking time to tell rumors of creatures that lurked in the darkness, that the things teasing at mankind's nightmares were all too real.

Sometimes he was joined by another, a quick-limbed woman in a long trench coat, the new leather supple and shiny. She flitted in and out, and from time to time he disappeared with her to places further than his feet could carry him. Once, when they reached a small town in the Midwest, she took a detour on her own to a blue house at the top of a hill. She teleported inside, navigating its halls with ease, passing an old picture of a young woman in a graduation robe, and another of that woman in a long white coat in front of a hospital. Upstairs she found a man and a woman sleeping, their hair much grayer now, their postures obviously stooped even in sleep. She stood watching them, brought here by a memory she had lied about not recovering, one she had glimpsed in a flash that night when she made her choice. A memory she had come to close.

The woman in the bed stirred and sat up, clearing her eyes. When she saw the figure at the foot of the bed, her eyes went wide and her mouth opened to scream, either in fear or joy, or a horrible combination of the two.

"Hush," Traveler said, as gently as a mother urging an infant back to sleep, raising a black-gloved hand to lips that had curled into a sad smile. The woman obeyed; the voice compelled her to, even as an invisible hand squeezed the life out of her heart, quick and painless, as merciful as possible.

Back in the grove, Thinker pondered and planned, their body fully healed and resplendent, proud in the rays of the sun. Soon it would be spring. And by then, Thinker would have more practice using their new skills, more practice working together with the group as one. In the meantime, the house moved itself to the left by five feet. Yesterday, it was three. And next week, in an instant, the house would find itself twenty yards closer to the road. Yes, soon spring would indeed come, that sacred time of renewal, and wherever their kind were, whatever dark roads they roamed without purpose or future, they would no longer roam it alone. They would look up and see a house there in front of them. Its majestic doors would open, welcoming them in, and a great assembly would enfold them, letting them know their time had come at last.

THE END?

Not if you want to dive into more of Crystal Lake Publishing's Tales from the Darkest Depths!

Check out our amazing website and online store or download our latest catalog here: https://geni.us/CLPCatalog.

We always have great new projects and content on the website to dive into, as well as a newsletter, behind the scenes options, social media platforms, our own dark fiction shared-world series and our very own webstore. Our webstore even has categories specifically for KU books, non-fiction, anthologies, and of course more novels and novellas.

AUTHOR BIOGRAPHY

C.L. Kelley is a horror author and musician who lives in the southeastern United States. She has previously released an anthology of short stories, *Uncanny Tales*, as well as three albums. This is her first published novel.

Readers…

Thank you for reading *Corpus*. We hope you enjoyed this novel. If you have a moment, please review *Corpus* at the store where you bought it.

Help other readers by telling them why you enjoyed this book. No need to write an in-depth discussion. Even a single sentence will be greatly appreciated. Reviews go a long way to helping a book sell, and is great for an author's career. It'll also help us to continue publishing quality books.

Thank you again for taking the time to journey with Crystal Lake's Torrid Waters.

You will find links to all our social media platforms on our Linktree page: https://linktr.ee/CrystalLakePublishing.

MISSION STATEMENT

Since its founding in August 2012, Crystal Lake Publishing has quickly become one of the world's leading publishers of Dark Fiction and Horror books. In 2023, Crystal Lake Publishing formed a part of Crystal Lake Entertainment, joining several other divisions, including Torrid Waters, Crystal Lake Comics, and many more.

While we strive to present only the highest quality fiction and entertainment, we also endeavor to support authors along their writing journey. We offer our time and experience in non-fiction projects, as well as author mentoring and services, at competitive prices.

With several Bram Stoker Award wins and many other wins and nominations (including the HWA's Specialty Press Award), Crystal Lake puts integrity, honor, and respect at the forefront of our publishing operations.

We strive for each book and outreach program we spearhead to not only entertain and touch or comment on issues that affect our readers, but also to strengthen and support the Dark Fiction field and its authors.

Not only do we find and publish authors we believe are destined for greatness, but we strive to work with men and women who endeavor to be decent human beings who care more for others than themselves, while still being hard-working, driven, and passionate artists and storytellers.

Crystal Lake is and will always be a beacon of what passion and dedication, combined with overwhelming teamwork and respect, can accomplish. We endeavor to know each and every one of our readers, while building personal relationships with our authors, reviewers, bloggers, podcasters, bookstores, and libraries.

This is what we believe in. What we stand for. This will be our legacy.

Welcome to Crystal Lake Entertainment.

Also from Torrid Waters...

Come for Thanksgiving Dinner. Stay for the Feast.

Sierra's first American Thanksgiving promises to be unforgettable when her college roommate, Zoe, invites her to the Samuels family feast. But as the ten-hour banquet unfolds, it becomes clear this is no ordinary holiday gathering.

With everyone bound by a chilling rule—eat and drink exactly as served, and enjoy it, or face dire consequences—the traditional celebration quickly takes a dark and macabre turn. Will Sierra survive the Samuels' sinister hospitality or become part of a feast far more horrifying than she could have ever imagined?

Question Not My Salt is a gripping tale blending the terror of *The Texas Chainsaw Massacre* with the culinary horror of *Hannibal* and *The Menu*.

Also from Torrid Waters...

A fast-paced story of survival, terror, family, and friendship.

The people of Wicker thought the mountain belonged to them—purchased with blood, sweat, and resilience. They forgot the deal their ancestors made. They forgot that their mountain belonged to something ancient, powerful, and hungry.

Charlotte Crowe and Rebecca Greenleigh grew up as best friends on the mountain, descendants of the original settlers of Wicker and inheritors of a terrible secret. They expected to grow old on their mountain. They did not expect the return of the wolves, the bone chimes appearing overnight in the trees, or their neighbors turning on one another. In a matter of days, everything they thought they knew is flipped upside down and they find themselves trapped in a place they once called home playing a dangerous game with a creature older than the mountain itself.

THANK YOU FOR PURCHASING THIS BOOK